Robert Brown

Tellis and Kleobeia

Robert Brown

Tellis and Kleobeia

ISBN/EAN: 9783337366551

Printed in Europe, USA, Canada, Australia, Japan

Cover: Foto ©Andreas Hilbeck / pixelio.de

More available books at **www.hansebooks.com**

BY

ROBERT BROWN, JUN., F.S.A.

'How small a part of time they share,
That are so wondrous sweet and fair!'
WALLER.

LONDON
·DAVID NUTT, 270-271, STRAND
1895

CONTENTS

TELLIS AND KLEOBEIA.

'WELCOME from Delphoi, my Deinomachê,
And tell your Myrô, who has stayed at home,
Though not forgetful of her comely Girl,
How thou hast sped, what seen, and if the god
Were gracious to thee.'

'Yes, indeed, dear Myrô ;
A time so sweet and so replete with peace,
So brightly grave, so joyously serene,
Lighted by thoughts whose ever sun-touched wings
Suggested glimpses of the eternal gods ;
By fancies not all fancy, but, as 'twere,
Echoes from far-off heights where morning reigns :—
By kindling aspirations that stretch forth
Their eager hands towards a hidden fount
Of beauty and of harmony ;—a time
Unruffled by the discord of the world,
Such was our stay at Delphoi.   King Apollôn,
Well may we reverence thee !'

A

'You have learnt much :
And did you mount in body as in soul
Towards the Twy-topped, climb with rising day,
Look Morning in the eyes and drink her breath,
And feel the rush of youth intensified?'

'Ay, dearest Myrô, when the Early Star
Paled in her place and fled to sacred Night,
We worshipped at the splendour of the Dawn;
And, gazing on her rosy-fingered grace,
Felt light-struck to the soul; the spirit of health,
The blood of freedom coursing through our veins.'

'The soul that's free is never far from heaven.'

'And we are free, dear Myrô. Athens, free,
Stands centre of the world. Wherever men
Are stirred by noble impulse to broad aims,
Which make for general good and brighten life,
They turn to Athens. All the Island-flowers,
Linked by our galleys in harmonious chain,
With holy Dêlos for its central point,—
Look to Athêna's city. Spear and shield
Against all tyrants, beautiful she stands!
For, Athens is Athêna upon earth;
And the high gods, who lend their store to man,
Grace her with gifts indeed. Supremest skill,

Arms without grimness, art that rivals heaven
In shrine and statue. And, around the whole,
A noble purpose brought to splendid close,—
The bulwarks of Themistoklês. Yet, stay,—
Pardon me, Myrô ; I had half forgot
You are not all Athenian.'

      ' No. My mother
Came from the wall-less City. But, go on,—
Go on, my pretty patriot. This outburst
Shows well in you ; perchance, it is inspired
By Loxias, whom you spoke of.'

      ' Well, my Myrô,
See how the Delphian pours his sacred flame
Upon our Athens. When the spring comes round,
And earth bursts forth in her eternal life,
Triumphant over winter, can the world
Show such a sight? The mighty City meets
Within the theatre-temple of the god,
To hear the latest message which unfolds
The past in words from heaven. O glorious souls
Who scatter through all hearts their glowing fires !
Athenians, Strangers, and Barbarians hear,
And work the noble echoes into life,
Which thus must grow in grandeur.'

       ' Are you sure ? '

'Yes.   Did not Athens like a phoenix rise
From out her ashes?   Let the Persian rest.
I thank him that he burnt her.   Did not she
Stand in the van and roll the spoiler back,
Despite his giant bulk and monstrous fame,
And save the West from bondage?   If to-day
Throughout our Hellas man is truly man,
And not a dumb and burden-bearing beast
Crouching beneath the whip of some slave's slave,
Whose master's master is the Great King's slave,
Then thank our Athens.'

'Yes, I thank her, Sweet;
Leônidas thanks Athens.'

'Oh, I know
The Spartan Lion was a glorious man,
And like a god he died!'

'Yes, he died well.
Go on, dear Child, and tell your Myrô more
Of Athens and her glories.   Am not I
A daughter of the golden grasshopper?'

'I thank the gods, my Myrô, that you are!
Oh, when I think there runs within our veins
Such blood as burned at Salamis, I feel
Athéna beckons Athens, bids advance

Towards the still more glorious.   Distant lands
Shall feel her light and leading, bow the neck,
And Athens reign in splendour.   E'en her girls
Are daughters of the men of Marathôn,
And that should make us queens.'

                       ' Democracies
Should not be fond of queens, Deinomachê.'

' All of us queens, dear Myrô, that is fair.'

' Fair queens, I doubt not, and it may be fair ;
For your Athenian democrat would place
Athenians first, then Strangers, then the World,—
Barbarians, as we term them ; and, it seems,
Of all Athenians not the last himself :
So that the freedom which he thus proclaims,
Is that himself should take the foremost place,
As doubtless is most fitting.   'Tis a creed
I've heard in Lakedaimôn.   Let it pass.'

' You seem to doubt of Athens.   Is it so ? '

' I do not doubt her glory or her skill,
More than I doubt thy love.   Her voice of song
Shall reach across the misty gulf of death,
Unsilenced by the ages.   Marathôn—
The very name is one with Glory's self,

And breathes a deathless music. Centuries
Pass into shadow, yet her sacred plain
In echo all undying shall preserve
The thunder of that onset. It may be
That fragments of our sculpture will be prized
By mighty nations of the time to come,
As presents worthy of a king to kings;
Whilst memories of our painters dominate
Their grandest efforts. An eternal fame
The gods bestow on Athens. Fear it not.'

' But, yet, you doubt of something?'

'Yes, I doubt

Of human justice. Is it well that we
Should govern others only for ourselves?
Blot out their power, and make them yield their
    gold;
And, thus, instead of gaining true allies,
Devoted to our cause, because our cause
Is theirs and freedom's, we are ringed with slaves,
Greek though they be, who, if the push of war
Should thrust us backward, would at once fly off
And side with our opponents. Is it well
That every idle ranter bawl and mouth
In endless iteration, catching fools
E'en greater than himself? Or, is it well

That jealousy of merit and of wealth,
Of name, and fame, and station, spits its hate
With ever thickening venom? That the tongue,
Brazen with lungs of leather, should roar down
Sense, knowledge, and experience? That the man
Who flatters most profoundly all around
With lavish proffers of still easier ways
To wealth and pleasure, should be trusted most?
That idleness should masquerade as toil?
Word-mongering pass for wisdom? Discontent
Pose as supremest virtue? Whilst, alas!
Old faith is passing, unreplaced by new,
And Zeus, some think, dismounted from his throne
By Dinos, or by atoms.'

        'Gods forbid.'

'Yes, they forbid, and Dinos shall not reign.
But, mark, Deinomachê, look round the world,
And tell me where can Athens find a friend,
Greek or Barbarian. Grim Lakônikê
Waits till the time is ripe. Some popular fool
Shall act a madness 'mid immense applause ;
Fritter our strength in senseless enterprise,
Enrage with insolence a hostile world,
And then——'

        'Our fleet shall keep that world at bay.'

' 'Tis bravely spoken. So, our one resource,
Our only shield and buckler is the fleet,
Which links a scattered empire, guards the bread
Sent us by distant lands, for Attikê
Cannot feed Athens. Should it chance our fleets
Were storm-tossed, or defeated, or betrayed
By their commanders—and such things might be—
What could avail your walls impregnable?
They need not be assailed; they would but prove
A ghastly tomb of famine.'

                         'Myrô, Myrô!'

'Well, my heart's love.'

                       'It is impossible
That such a glorious empire, queen o' the seas,
Splendour of arts and arms, great roll of fame,
Vanguard of progress, strong in east and west,
Should stoop to ruin. Though the banded might
Of all our foemen thundered to the charge,
Persian, and Spartan, and Korinthian,
Boiôtian, and Barbarian of the North—
Pallas the Stormer, Promachos, the First
In battle's tempest, she would smite them down
As erst she smote huge Arês.'

                        'Did she save
The sacred towers of Ilion, though a queen,

And Troian matrons, wailing in her shrine,
Besought Athêna's mercy with rich gift?'

'Athens enslaved!   It is impossible!
Firm-rooted earth would stagger, and the Powers
Of heaven be shaken.   She shall stand and reign,
The guiding star of this majestic world:
Her gods, her men will save her.'

                'Did the gods
That ruled the destinies of Babylôn,
Chaldaean Zeus upon his golden seat,
With all the armament of heaven, defend
From Mede or Persian?   When the time was ripe
And the State rotten, e'en Aigyptos fell.
And what availed her wisdom and her work,
Her pyramids and temples?   Did Osiris,
Isis, or Ammôn bar the spoiler's way?
Oh, there are gods and gods, as men and men,
Outworn and fallen as old Kronos fell;
Or deaf, and dead, and angered.   For when man
Casts the choice gifts of heaven beneath his feet,
Calls licence liberty, deems madness wise,
Builds temples but believes not, boasts of freedom
Whilst slave to myriad follies, scoffs at justice,
And worships but himself; then those high Powers
That sit serene in splendour, and direct
The onward of the world, from Erebos,

Summon to sunlight that tremendous form,
Erinys, the Gloom-haunter, to avenge
Insulted goodness.   So, Deinomachè,
Doubting of human justice, I must fear
Justice divine, and all the chance of Time,
Which wears the marble, dries the fertile brain,
Eats the heart out of prudence, saps the strength
Of resolution, and makes man a child,
With no sweet promise of a youth to come.'

' You make my heart bleed. Do you love our Athens?'

' I love your Athens, she is also mine ;
I love her so, I would not live an hour
When she had spent her freedom ; yet I hold
The dice of Zeus can never fall amiss:
He reigns, and he shall reign ; as erst they sang :
Zeus was, Zeus is, Zeus will be.   O great Zeus!
So, if our orb of glory, which aspires
To starry lustres, sink in western gloom
And depths Kimmerian ; if the hand of Time
Topple our Parthenon, and break the spear
Which flashes light to Sounion ; if we pass
Like Tiryns, or like Troia, pass to dream,—
A faded glory of the earlier time,
A quarry for the poet, an example
For grave philosophers to warn mankind

Against our faults and follies ; be it so.
Greatness is greater than the greatest man,
Beauty more beauteous ; the divine ideal,
Mirrored in depths of the pellucid soul,
Shall still in tranquil motion, whilst at rest,
Pass towàrds heights diviner.   God will reign
Without our prayers and praise : we should not speak
As though He needed anything ; new babes
Sprung from our mother Earth shall lisp and play,
And grow towards the stature of a man,
Or even of a god.   The final end
Does not depend on Athens, heaven forbid !
For, even as man dies, but still the world
Glows in fresh beauty ; so, a tribe, a race,
A special force, singular excellence,
Great deeds achieving, wonders to themselves,
And e'en to others, must in tract of time
Sink like a stone in ocean.   It may leave
Remembrance, influence, guiding, warning voice,
May help to shape the future ; but itself
Is gone, and that for ever.   Only men
Deem themselves so important, stretch their necks
To touch that ceiling where the starry chiefs
Dart from their eyes the flaming rays of fire,
And almost think to reach it, that 'tis well
In sober sadness we should recollect
Our true position.   Be we what we may,

We can be cast aside and never missed
By that infinitude of force and thought,
Purpose, and progress, and material stuff
Which makes the world and gods. And, thus, although
If Athens perished, I would stretch mine arms
To Power diviner in the darkness veiled,
And say, O Father, take your child ; yet still,
Passing or tarrying, I should not despair
Of ultimate achievement. The same stars
Would smile upon the world ; the selfsame hope
That lights the soul, would hold her torch un-
    dimmed ;
The same majestic Love whose silent voice
Soothes into-rest the myriad babes of Time,
And bids them sleep untroubled, still would end
The anguish of the moment, bid the storm
Pass, and be swallowed in divine repose.'

' Yes, dearest Myrô, but I cannot think
Of earth without our Athens.'

                        ' No, my Child,
Nor need you ; but to me the greatest joy,
The basis of all harmony is this,—
That, through the shocks and tossings of our life,
We can discern the workings of a Power
Making for good, with infinite resolve

And matchless steadfastness; it labours not
As we would have it, because gods and men
Are different; and, if it worked as we,
And we could trace such working, we should know,
To our immense confusion, that the course
Of nature and of period was arranged
By some poor mind, another of ourselves,
Weakling to breed confusion and dismay,
As Phaëthôn in the chariot of the sun.
Therefore, that all the glittering web of life
Is something tangled, does not seem to reach
A lucid end, and weave its pattern plain ;
But, like the garment of Pênelopê,
Begins anew, and puzzles us who wait
At threshold of the gods, dismays me not.
For, if Zeus reign, as reigns he, then I know
That Dinos, whom some vaunt of, cannot be,
Save as the phantom of a feeble brain,
And shadow of a shade.   Therefore, Deinomaché,
If we despond of Athens, we will strive,
However little we can say or do,
To help her in her need.   If Athens fail,
There is the world, with all its hope and good,
And future of development.   If that
Sink into chaos, yet, behind all strife,
Failure, pain, passion, punishment and loss,
There stands eternal God.   But, tell me now

Of what you saw at Delphoi. Let us leave
These graver fancies, these Eumenides
That dog our fearful minds ; and, at the shrine
Of many garlands, where the healing Seer,
Loxias, the true diviner, will protect
All suppliants at his marble navel-stone,
Take refuge ; and prefer our prayer, and honour
The ancient custom of the tripod. Now
We will approach in spirit, cleanse our souls ;
For holy places of the blessed gods
Are open to the Good. A single drop
Of water is an ocean in their cause ;
But the whole sacred rivers and the seas
Will fail the Evil : as the Pythia asked,
Man shall a wetted body wash thy soul?
Then tell me, Sweet, of Delphoi. We will sit
Beside the Priestess, hear her gracious words ;
And, if the days are somewhat dark and dim,
Heed her bold counsel, *Counterstrike the coin,*
When flatterers and panders would debase
Image and superscription.'

            ' Well, then, Myrô,
On the eastern front of the temple I beheld,
Wrought into subtle semblance, two great deeds
Of superhuman daring. Hêraklês,
His vast frame strung in one immense resolve—

Hewed at the Hydra's horror.   Every stroke
The golden falchion made lopped off a head,
Whilst Iolaos, with his blazing brand,
Burnt the foul thing to an eternal death,
And so they conquered.   Did they thus contend?'

'What said your nurse?'

                  'She told me that they did;
And said that when the fight was at the worst,
A giant Crab, emerging from the lake,
Crawled to the fiend's assistance, bit the foot
Of Hêraklês, and added to his pains.
But do you think it?'

                'Have you never seen
That crab at night, Deinomachê?'

                    'Why, no;
How should I see it?'

                'Then, look up on high,
When shines the Lion with his kingly star;
And you shall see the memory of that fight
Emblazoned in the heavens.   The Lion-heart
Wrapped in the lion-skin, falchion in hand—
Men call it now the Sickle—rushes on
Against the hostile, dark, opposing Crab,
And tramples Hydra underneath his feet.'

'Oh, now I know. Why, then, the tale is true;
And Hêraklês slew Hydra, did he not?'

'He may have done for aught thy Myrô knows;
Or there may lurk a meaning in the tale
Which Myrô can but guess at. Well, then,
    Sweet,
What saw you next?'

                          'Vaulting Bellerophôn

On winged charger, slaying with his shafts
The Triple-creature, lion, snake, and goat.
Were there such monsters?'

                          'Monsters were and are;

And heroes must oppose them, ay, and will.
For king Apollôn, lord of light and law,
Whose shrine is that of Themis, undertakes
Through all the valliant brotherhood of man,
And through his own ineffable, divine
Enforcement of the will of highest Zeus,
This contest through the ages. The tried souls
That stand around his altar, must contend
With dread Chimairas in fire-breathing might,
And slay by shafts of splendour, soar to heaven,
Perchance to fall, though only for a time,
Bruised to the heart, it may be; never again

To rise triumphant in this lower world,
But limping on to Acherôn.'

                ' Then I saw

The War of Gods and Giants. Pallas, first,
Brandished her shield against Enkelados,
And tumbled him to ruin. O, I read
A meaning in the picture. Athens there
Rolled back the Mede to Hadês.'

                'So, you see,
These pictures and these stories may be true
In many variant ways ; may represent
The physical, the immaterial,
The contest of the soul, the shocks of time,
The passage of the ages, and unseen
Yet vast realities which ring us round.
What next beheld you ?'

                'Why, our father Zeus
Blasting huge Mimas into ashes. Next,
Was Dionysos, with his thyrsos armed,
Smiting down Eurytos ; and all these forms
Lived without motion and in silence spoke.'

'How marvellous the link 'twixt shape and
      soul !

                        B

Form springing from the formless, chain which binds
Rapture with horror.   And you passed within?'

'Yes, and saw all the treasure; the huge bowl
Of silver which the cunning Samian made;
Homêros' statue, and an iron chair
Of Pindaros, wherein he hymned the god;
A triple-headed serpent that supports
The golden tripod by the altar; this
Recording how our Hellas crushed the Mede;
The gold and silver vases Kroisos sent;
The statues of the dual Destinies,
With their great lord and leader, father Zeus,
And king Apollôn, who directs them too.'

'Yes, for Apollôn ever manifests
In harmony and light the mind of Zeus,
And spreads his message to the outmost world.
So, when our Hellenes drive their daring keels
Through seas unknown, seeking remotest shores,
Apollôn is the patron of their toil,
And guides and guards our colonists.   The shrine
You might not enter.'

                        'No.   By special grace
I was allowed to question; so I knelt
Without, and made my offering: and they said

That the great Priestess, with her far-off eyes,
And laurel-crownèd brows, upon the tripod,
Her throne majestic, filled with the divine,
Replied as one who echoes distant light:

Deinomachê, have a care. Thou art mortal to run
*　　with immortals :*
Speed as a Penthesileia ; no lingering stoop. Ata-
*　　lanta*
Lost by a glitter of gold ; but, the Bride who would
*　　mother a lion—*
Rest at the last shall be hers, in the beautiful grove of
*　　the poplar.*

'Thus spake she, and I trembled.'

　　　　　　　　　　　　' Do not fear ;
Zeus and Apollôn are the highest Fates ;
And all the seeming discord of the world
Is man's misreading of their melody,
In partial comprehension : bounded gaze
Which draws fresh errors from its ignorance,
And staggers through its strength '

　　　　　　　　　　　' Beside her stands
The statue of Apollôn, all of gold.
Why prize we gold, my Myrô ?'

' Has not he
Whose chair was shown you, told us?   Is not gold
A glory of the Sun-god ?   *Shining far*
Above all wealth, as through the dark of night
Shines blazing flame ; and, thus, Hyperiôn's bride,
Theia divine, the mother of the Sun,
Is golden Chrysê ; and, around the god,
In his own sacred seat, as risen light,
Are ringed the splendours which proclaim his
     sway ;
Art earthly thus reflecting art divine.'

' Then came I forth, and other things I saw ;
The grave of Neoptolemos, and, near,
The stone of ancient Kronos.'

          ' Poor old god !
Type of the rude and all-imperfect world,
Savage in its disorder ; in unrest
Passed into darkness, and for ever bound
Beneath unvintaged ocean and the earth,
Thus making way for calm. And did you note
The pictures Thasian Polygnôtos wrought ? '

' O, yes, my Myrô, to the right and left
In majesty upon the Leschê's walls,
Above Kassôtis' fountain. You have seen them ? '

'Yes, I have seen them. There stand life and death
And death in life, and life victorious,
Passing through death and shadow to the dawn
Of what is fadeless. Did you mark them well?'

'I gazed upon them long; but I am young,
With little knowledge of this boundless world,
Except its brightness; yet, within mine eyes
Rose unsuspected tears, I know not why.'

'Because, Deinomachê, thou didst perceive,
However dimly, the vast war and wail
Of souls, or clothed or naked, as they pass
Through the great halls of the eternal shrine,
Sun-lighted or obscured. Didst mark the names?'

'Some of the mourning Ilian sisterhood,
Andromachê, with fatherless boy babe;
Mêdesikastê and Polyxena,
Sad choir of beauty smitten into dust;
Whilst Helenê, triumphant through all change,
Is seated more than queen. And the great heroes-
Aias, Odysseus, Neoptolemos,
I noted these and others.'
     'You beheld
Not merely Troia's daughters and her sons,
Trampled by feet Hellenic, the vast prize

Of an immortal contest; but the dream
Which men call mortal life, depicted fair,
With but few colours : for, the chords which form
The staple of its song are ever few,
And yet their variant combinations reach
Towards infinity.   O 'tis a harp
Of unexhausted powers, on which men play
With petty skill, and deem the strings out worn ;
Because their touch is dull, their fingers cramped
With narrowing imitation.   So all greatness
Makes myriad puny prettinesses rise
And pipe but for a day.   Patience and wait :
The hours roll by ; the subtly-working gods
Hear the hymn quavering into littleness ;
And, when the time is fully ripe, produce
Their hidden singer from the light of heaven :
Then every chord thrills music fresh and free,
Whilst the glad volume of exulting song
Soars starward, lighting up the azure steeps
With pure and fragrant fires.'

                                  'But life is sad,
My Myrô.'

            'Yes, unutterably sad,
As Polygnôtos shows us in his work,
By what he paints and paints not.   Love makes grief ;

Hektór is dead, and sad Andromachê,
Longing for death, is stayed by baby hands,
Whose gentle touch makes life so terrible
With vistas of fresh woes.   Then you would turn,
From life to life, and scan the other side?'

' Yes, and I love that painting on the left,
With its dim shadowy terrors, and its lights
Shining through darkness.   But, come, tell me,
    Myrô,
For what I saw, I saw not as I ought,
About this mighty picture of the shades,
Its mystery and its meaning, you are wise.'

' Wise am I, my Deinomachê?   Alas!
Before these tragic and triumphant depths,
With all their infinite suggestiveness
Of hope and fear, of past and of to come,
Thy Myrô's wisdom shrivels to a speck.
She bows herself before the infinite pain
And pity of our being; veils her face
Before its grandeur and colossal calm;
And lowers her eyes, half blinded by its hopes,
Sparkling in lightning glimpses through a veil,
The peplos of Harmonia.   As a maid
Stands in the presence of some mighty king,
And feels his burning eyes devour her soul;

But, yet, through all her terror and her awe,
Is irresistibly drawn, as moth to flame,
With rapture-tinted fear ; so, I behold
This work of Polygnôtos, vaster far
Than Polygnôtos dreamed of, when he clad
The sacred legends of the earlier time
In palpable form.'

'And are these stories true?'

'The stories are most true, Deinomachê ;
But Truth has many sides and many shapes.
With what can we compare it ?   What is Truth?
Suffice we know it somewhat : let it be
The harmony of Being and Belief.
And, as the Thasian painted, first of all,
The tale of Troia—tale of mortal life ;
So, now he limns the vaster scene beyond
With figures protagonistic, who unfold
A rhythmic progress of the eternal Soul,
Upward, some call it, downward, others : I
Shall name it onward.   And, Deinomachê,
Mark, the two pictures have a special link,
The much-achieving, much-enduring Man,
Who, having toiled through sunlight, dares the gloom
To seek a Soul more perfect, and to know
Of home and his return.   Tell me, ye depths,
Rich with experience and diviner types

Of man and woman than the sun beholds;
With prophet-kings, seers, in eye and mind,
Freed from their mortal darkness, and who move
Godlike 'mid ghosts ; tell me, great treasure-house
Of buried wisdom and of holy aims,
Stored with the loves of all the ages past,
Temple of pause, whose dimly-lighted halls
Encircle forms majestic ; crypt divine,
Rare casket, far more wondrous than the work
Wrought by Héphaistos, and replete with gems,
Whose lustre through their sombre setting gleams ;
Tomb of fled hope, which all the myriad souls
That Hermês leads adown the shadowed ways,
Can never fill ; tell me, dread Oracle,
Where is my home? What! Is Teirésias silent ? '

' I am half frightened, Myrô, at your look.
You gaze as if you saw the Theban stand,
And beckon with his sceptre.'

       ' Pardon, Sweet ;
Recall me to the picture.'

         ' Yes, I will.
I marked Odysseus kneeling with drawn sword
Over the trench, and near the Theban sage
Is Antikleia, seated on a stone,
Patiently waiting.'

'As Homêros tells:
When prince Teirêsias passed within the house,
Odysseus still stood steadfast; and the soul
Of Antikleia drew nigh, and drank the blood:
And then she knew him, and she wept aloud,
And said, My Child, that art a living man,
How cam'st thou 'neath the darkness and the shade?
For dread is Hadês to the living sight,
With mighty rivers, aye, and dreadful streams
Between our realm and man's. And he replied,
O mother, of necessity I came
To seek Teirêsias. Tell me of my wife:
And then her spirit told him, and she said,
'Twas not the archer goddess of keen sight
Who slew me with her shafts; wasting disease
Drew not the spirit from my limbs; I died
Of my sore longing once to see thy face,
And hear again thy counsel and thy love.'
Thus spake she. You remember he replied:
'*I stood and mused; the purpose of my soul*
Was to embrace my mother's spirit. Thrice
I did attempt it: thrice betwixt my hands
She flitted as a shadow or a dream,
And ever sharper heart-pang I endured.
My mother, wailed I, wherefore dost thou fly,
Thy son who fain would grasp thee? That e'en
       here

In Hadês, we might cast our loving arms
Each about each, and satiate our woe.
O glorious scene of love! Stronger than death,
Deeper than darkness, true as truth itself,
Spurning at peril, triumphing in pain,
And trampling into nothing mortal fears!'

'I was but little when my mother died,
But I remember with how keen a pain
I saw all life flow on ; suns rose and set,
And tiny children played and crowed, and girls
Rippled in laughter ; whilst the whole hard world
Paused not an instant for a single prayer,
But rolled remorseless onwards ; and I felt
An anger and a hate against my kind,
Burning to break in torrent of wild speech,
Upbraiding and accusing. But it failed ;
And, "Mother," "Mother !" I could say no more.'

'So, then, I came, Deinomachê.'

'You did ;
And all my mother seemed seemed to live in you.
But, if I ever see her face again,
And clasp her to my soul, I'll tell her this :
That you have mothered her poor, desolate Girl
Made my life bright with perfume of sweet love,

Sheltered me in your bosom; and, when she,
The mother I have lost, hears all my tale,
She will stretch forth fair hands of welcoming,
And take you to her heart, whilst all the place
Shall echo music.   Oh, that I might know!'

' Am I Teirésias to resolve your doubt?
Ask not, dear child, let the bright Nymphs of Time
Chase through the zodiac.   There will be a goal.
Now, tell me of some other forms you saw.'

'Nigh the dim river, sitting on a skin
Of some foul bird, and gnashing hateful fangs,
With black-blue tint, like meat-infesting fly,
Crouches the fiend Eurynomos.   He eats,
The Delphians told us, flesh from dead men's
      bones.
Mysterious horror! is there such a thing?'

'Surely there is.   The open maw of Death;
Eurynomos, the Universal law—
Sarkophagos, corruption's hideous tooth,
Which fastens on these vestures of decay
That clothe our souls; but nothing worse than
      this.'

' I thank the gods.'

'Sweet, fear no animate fiend.
No Kerberos has Polygnôtos drawn,
And Kerberos is but Darkness—as a dog
That guards the house of Hadês.   Still, your eye
Would notice divers pain-tormented souls.'

'There I beheld the shadow of a shade,
Dim in colossal bulk—huge Tityos,
Pain-shattered into weakness infinite,
Recumbent in a sleep, deeper than death.'

'Awful offender!   Awful chastisement!
Yet, even here, storm passes at the last,
And leaves behind a dull and dreamless peace
Freed from all pang, which haply pitying Time
May ripen into pardon.'

                    'There I saw
Sad Tantalos in grievous torment held;
Standing in water nigh unto the chin,
In agony to drink.   The treacherous wave
Illudes him ever.   O'er his agèd head
A huge stone threatens; almost in his reach
Tall trees display their beauty with bright fruit,
Pears, apples, and pomegranates, olives, figs.
His eager hands would clutch them; they are gone
As if wind-swept into the shadowy clouds!
'Tis terribly depicted.'

'And most true.'

'Lived he not once in Asia?'

'So they say!
He also lives in Athens, or at Thebes,
And grasps at phantom pleasure. Youth grows
    old,
Life stale, hope dead, and nature all out worn,
Yet still he gasps and clutches, thirsts again.'

'There is a hill, and wretched Sisyphos
The huge stone gripping, in his vain attempt,
With dusty head, sweat pouring from his limbs.'

'And thus we learn, Deinomachê, that they,
Who through this mortal circle of our life
Pursue the more ignoble, eat and drink,
As death-doomed on the morrow, may be cursed
In the hereafter with the dreadful fate
To seek this still, oblivious of aught else;
Seek it, yet never find, unsatisfied
In horrible soul-hunger evermore.'

'Then there is painted Oknos making rope,
Which a she-ass devours as soon as made;
And the Guide said his wife consumed his
    wealth.'

' Let him not be thy guide.   Such silly tales
Befit an empty showman.   Oknos sits
All dull and sluggish, labouring blindly on
To find the truth of things; with method
    none,
Nor aught of knowledge, or of holy fear;
But, stung to morbid energy by dim
Dissatisfaction, which can see the worse,
The discord and the shadow, and no more.
Stupidity, with her triumphant bray,
Engulfs his effort perishing still-born.'

' And then I saw the water-bearers toil,
Emptying their vessels in a mighty jar.'

' A task impossible.   'Tis Tantalos
In variant aspect; uninitiate souls,
Danaides for ever, cannot fill
The wine-jar of their appetites, constrained
To use but broken pitchers for the task;
And trickle tiny streams into a gulf
Insatiable as Hades.   The wise man
Commends the middle.   *Nothing in excess.*'

' Then, Myrô, it is good that we should know
The secrets of Eleusis?'

'Truly, yes;
For her high ritual doth as far surpass
All other forms of service, as the gods
Are more than heroes.   What saith Pindaros?
Happy is he who knows these sacred rites
Ere 'neath the earth he passes.   Well he kens
Both of life's goal and of its source from heaven.
But what of all the heroes and the queens
Who dwell beyond the sun-gates and the flow
Of Ocean, in the mead of asphodel,
And whom our Thasian painter has portrayed?
People of dreams, a galaxy of souls
Across that river which is full of reeds.'

'There I marked Orpheus sitting on a hill;
His left hand held the harp, and with his right
He touched the branches of a willow-tree;
And I was glad to think not even Death
Can silence music.'

'No, indeed, dear Heart;
The shadowy Hadès has not lulled his lyre.
But, think not gloomily of Death.   He comes,
And with him his twin brother Sleep.   They bare
The mortal sufferer, seamed with many scars,
From out the dust and tumult of the world;
Bathe him within the river, then anoint

His head with sweet ambrosia, and clothe
His form in garments never growing old.
And as to this rare minstrel, you have seen
The zenith harp of Orpheus in the skies ;
And here in Hadês his triumphant hand
Is laid upon the willows of the queen,
To show that Orpheus and Persephonê
On earth, in heaven, and in the Underworld,
Make but one music in divine accord,
And light-revealing shadow. Melody,
Enchanting mirror of a world unseen,
Whispers and breathes of inconceivable
Supernal heights and splendours, till the soul
Views Êôs rise on noon. It is not dumb
Within the mead of asphodel, which speaks
The coming of a spring, the dawn of hope,
The flight of winter, and a burst of song,
With harmony unchecked by mortal tears.'

'Majestic forms are gathered round his harp ;
The sceptred Agamemnôn, and by him,
Antilochos whom goodly Memnôn slew,
Prôtesilaos gloriously loved,
Supreme Achilleus with his golden locks,
Patroklos standing by him. On the left
Leans Promedôn against a willow tree,
The Phôkian Schedios, king Pelias,

c

The hoary-headed, gazing at the harp;
And luckless Thamyris with broken lyre,
Dejected on the earth.'

'When this poor world
Thinks its own music, wild and meaningless,
Degraded passion vaunting of itself,
Can match the rhythmic harmonies of heaven,
And dares to challenge gods, beneath the stress
And storm of such a contest the weak chords
Of mortal harps are sundered, and song dies
In darkness and confusion. Marsyas
Distorts the features with his double pipe,
Clouds the serene with fumes of earthliness,
And suffers for presumption. So, too, Dance,
Song's sister, which the race of mortals love,
Is seemly or unseemly, as the mind
Of him who dances. Foolish Hippokleidês
Danced off his marriage : king Apollôn leads
His choir with stately step, and thus preserves
All dignity and freedom. Lyre and voice
And form should blend together, three in one,
A triple harmony. Pythagoras
Taught music is the link which binds the
     whole
Orderly unity, confusion's death ;
Not like that dance, *The Burning of the World.*'

' By Thamyris sits Hektôr, bowed with woe.'

'Self-love, self-will, twin mothers of all pain.
The image of an unforgotten past,
Unseemly or rebelled against, 'tis this
Makes the true darkness.   Noble Hektôr wait
In patience till the ripple dies away,
And all of pain has faded into light.'

'Then next was Memnôn, seated on a stone,
Sarpedôn with him; and upon his cloak
Were seen those sacred birds, whose holy wings
Sprinkle with dew his Hellespontine tomb.'

'Son of the Morning, fallen to the depths!
But yet to rise immortal; second he
To none except Pêleidês.'

                     ' Then the Maids,
Pandareôs' daughters, whom the Harpies snatched
And bore to the Erinyes, crowned with flowers,
Sat playing with their dice.   I deemed it strange.'

'And it is strange, Deinomachê; and much
That mighty minds have wrought is passing strange;
Because it is an outcome of that vast
Unknown of wonder and immortal thought

Which rings our souls.   The fragments we behold
We cannot join together; nor restore
The pattern of the peplos of the world
From these rent pieces; so the whole design
Outstrips intelligence.   Give us the claw,
And we can form the lion; but the course
Of Nature and of Destiny involves
An unimagined grandeur, speaks a depth
Abysmal, infinite in space and time,
Which all our puny plummets cannot sound.
And   hence   these   flaming   fragments,   these   bright
    thoughts—
Cast from some central fire upon the earth
To burn in certain souls—detached from truths
We never heard of, seem, in severed form,
At times unworthy of their place; at times
Obscure and doubtful, as the grey-eyed peep
Of a dim dawn.   And every poet fails
To utter half his meaning, to convey
His broader purpose; and beholds his work,
Picture, or song, or statue, when complete,
Not as he dreamed it, but, as touched by earth;
A faint impression of a thought divine
Which died 'neath human handling.   Yonder scene
Is not what Polygnôtos in his dreams
Saw with delight, but all that man could do
To make his dream apparent to the world.'

'And yet it is most god-like.'

'So it is,
Compared with other failures; we will listen
To what he tells us as an oracle,
Cloudy, but splendour gleaming through the cloud.
And does not Palamêdês play at dice?'

'With Salaminian Aias and Thersitês.'

'I thought he was so painted.   Thus we note
That the wise hero and the innocent maids
Alike are players, and alike would see
The hazard of the future.   Dice are sacred
To Dionysos of the Underworld ;
Fall as they may, man's fate is sacred too,
And Klytiê and Kamirô snatched away,
Or Palamêdês drowned, or Aias spoiled
Of victory and glory, in their fates
And seeming failures, aye, and agonies,
Show certain numbers on the golden dice
Which fall from heaven upon the board o' the world :
For, as the wise have said, the whole profound
Is harmony and number intertwined ;
And number is the element of all
Diversity, which severs fate and fate ;
Yet every fate from heaven, fast sweeping on

To infinite fulfilment, and a time
When the seven Wandering Stars shall meet in light.
So, when these numbers point to loss, the wise
Possess their souls in patience ; place the game
In the high gods' own hands.   The baser sort
Pour vainly feverish vows ; and the dread dice
Whose counterparts the reckless gamester casts,
Gleaming and leaping, now above, below,
Fall on the board like fatal fires from heaven.
Handless they quell the strongest, cold they burn,
Pricking and paining with avenging goad ;
And oft, in dread deception, honey-tipped,
Allure by false success ; as Pentheus fell—
Polykratês, the victim of the Mede,
Shunned by the wise Amâsis ; type of man
Led headlong by avenging destinies.
And you would mark the noble ladies there ?'

' Yes, Thyia, Chlôris, Klymenê, and more ;
Kallistô with her bearskin ; Nomia
And Pérô, child of Neleus—group of flowers.'

' Ah, still they bloom, and winter fades in spring !
Lily, and rose, and moist anemone,
Tender narcissus, purple hyacinth,
The crocus-flame, and violets white and blue,
With myrtle of our Kypris ; iris last,

That links the earth with heaven. Plucked by stern
   hand,
Like the dread Queen herself, they root again ;
And, with their fragrant splendours, shed perfume
Down the dim years of troublous aftertime,
And make all Hadês smile.'

                   ' I noted, too,
Our father Thêseus by Peirithoös
Seated on rock enchanted, with sad gaze
Upon their useless swords which Thêseus holds.'

' Ah, frantic love of Beauty ! Love's own death !
Peirithoös, in counsel peer of gods,
His more than mortal wisdom valueless
Beneath the gust of passion, dared to raise
Wild, amorous eyes towards Persephonê,
So, to his earthly spirit grew the earth,
And clasped resistless fetter. Hêraklês,
They say, released our Thêseus, who had braved
In a sublime false friendship, endless wrath.
'Tis a dread tale ; I cannot read it plain.
Let such things be ; these riddles may be solved
By some Immortal when the years are passed,
And Time has sunk to Kronos.
But, tell me, Dearest, which of all the forms
Whose solemn splendours beckon to our gaze

Across the mist-enveloped gulf of death,
These poems of the past, whose souls intense
Have left deep tracks of grandeur, awful shades,
Or terrible, or beauteous, or instinct
With Melancholy's self; which most appealed
To your imagination or your heart?'

'I marvelled that through all the stately throng
Of those who did not suffer, man with man
Consorted, as did woman with her sex;
And man and woman did not seem to meet
But twice within the picture. It was strange.'

'Why strange, Deinomaché?'

'Because, my Myrô,
Does not their meeting strike the sweetest chords
That thrill our being? Is the after life
Grander than this if Love be left behind?'

'Who told thee Love was left? But, is there room
For Love's bright wings in Charôn's gloomy boat?'

'O, yes, my Myrô, yes, indeed there was.
I marked Penthesileia with her bow,
A star of battle, how she stood and scorned
Effeminate Paris. All her dainty shape
Rich with the vigour of the tireless wind,

And stormful independence; then I turned
To the dim stream of Acherôn, with its reeds
And gliding ghosts of fishes indistinct.
Lo, there, within the very boat itself,
The vessel of old Charôn, gaunt and grim,
Sat peacefully unconquerable love;
Tellis the youth, the virgin Kleobeia,
Dêmêtêr's sacred coffer on her knees.
But who they were I know not.'

        'Did you ask?'

'Yes, and our guide repeated what I saw,
That Tellis was a youth, and Kleobeia
A maiden who had lived and who had died.'

'Brief summary of a sunbeam! So it was.
Fair Morning star in this supernal world,
She shines the same, an evening star below.'

'Well, but, dear Myrô, tell me how they came
To gain a place in that tremendous scene,
Immortalised together. Were they lovers?
I know they were, and when I saw that Death
Failed to divide their beauty and their love,
And Darkness smiled upon them, oh, I felt
Such strange, sad pleasure! The heroic throng
Faded from sight, and all the shadowy scene

Passed into nothing; river, reeds, and fish,
Became as though they were not, and I said:
Tellis and Kleobeia happy still!'

' Eros have mercy on Deinomachê,
Already bound in fetters though so young,
Enamoured of no Tellis, but of Love,
The very god himself.   Yet you are right
To fix upon this couple.   Polygnôtos,
A Thasian, honouring a Thasian youth,
And the bright maiden who enriched his Isle
With holiest worship, placed the innocent pair
By kings and queens in Hadês.'

'He did well.'

'Yes, he did well; and when the deathless gods
Permit the mortal poet—he who makes—
Apollôn's workman—makes the unseen Good,
Give of its beauty, picture, verse or thought,
Thus to do well, the splendour of his work
Shines far beyond his ken; his magic urn,
Dipped in eternal fountains, pours a stream
To brighten lands that he has never known.
For all true song has, twined around its soul,
Significances infinite to arouse
Still vaster echoes in the aftertimes

From mighty hearts that follow; as a fire
Which from a hill-top speaks of coming war.
Sets twenty beacons blazing through the night.
Therefore the stars are numberless, and song
Is chorus, and all solitude is loss.
And, as it chances, I have by me here
A scroll in which some bygone poet sings
Of Tellis and the Maiden of his soul,
And how they loved and died.'

                 ' Read it, my Myrô ;
And let me nestle by you as you read :
So put your soft hand close around my neck,
Give me one kiss, and tell me all the tale.'

Then Myrô, a fair smile of guardian love,
Stooped down and kissed her; and in low, sweet
     voice,
That caught the flying fragrance of the past,
Pierced to its inmost meanings, lent it strength,
And clothed it with new beauty, thus began :—

At Thasos, where the Sun-god spreads his gold,
And Dionysos, lord of eastern lands,
Cheers mortals with the vine; the Isle which shows
An ass's backbone overspread by wood,
So huge Ipsariôn rises, crowned with firs—
Thasos of yore, haunt of Phoinikian men,
Who overturned a mountain in their greed—
Ringed by the blue Aigaion, Tellis dwelt.
On him our mother Nature had bestowed
A dower of potent beauty; supple limb,
And form a balance of harmonious grace,
With nothing lacking, nothing in excess,
Compact in easy vigour; such a man
As makes man know that he has sprung from gods,
And borrowed of their splendour: for, of a truth,
In intricate, mysterious unison,
The gleaming stairs that lead from heaven to earth
And downward to all depths, are marked by form
In variant divergence; till at base
Light's shadow, mind's distortion, Nature's trick,
Sits grinning, on the skin of a foul bird,
In blue-black horror, phantom of the gloom,
Eurynomos, the fiend.   Nor did a soul,
Unworthy of its stately dwelling-house,
Shine through the eyes of Tellis: gentle, pure,
Tender, and true, and trusting, yet, at times,

Enwrapped with sadness, like a lonely star,
In melancholy of its sweetness bred.
For the gods' open hands that shake out good
O'er earth and sea, and fill the heart of man
With plenty, and rejoice the patient beast,
And all innumerous life, drop into souls
Of rarest tissue, through their gifts a pain
Vague, and unformed, and indefinable,
Which still suggests, and spurs, and elevates,
And stimulates, and quickens, till it breeds
Divine dissatisfaction.   Hence, in strain
And doubt and agony, wrestling with Fate,
But overcoming by unceasing toil,
Is formed the Hero, and heroic work
Which joins men with the gods.   This golden
    link
Assists to knit the crawling human heart,
That tends towards Hadês in its impotence,
With the eternal centres of all light.

                    Such a pain
Slid through the soul of Tellis, undefined,
Yet palpable in its obscurity ;
Not common thought of shadowy life and death,
Not youth's spring yearning for a tender maid,
No zeal to rise and grasp the gauds of Time,
Nor carking care, pale child of penury ;

But a wish ever present in the soul,
At times a joy, at times an agony,
To penetrate into the heart o' the world;
To spread immortal wings and soar towards Truth,
Latent within the infinite obscure;
To touch the inner essence, find it heaven,
And gain its love for aye; to see a dawn
Rise on the morning, showing day in day,
And light of light, and clasp it evermore.
From these dim soul-hopes to the outward world,
Orderly splendour in activity,
Whose progress is the choric song of the gods—
The deep-eyed Tellis turned.   Can we by gaze,
Divine-illumined, search the very heart
Of Nature's mystery?   Rise to the springs
Whence gush the vital forces of the Seen,
And fill our mortal urn till it o'erflow
With the pure wave of the unfailing stream
Êridanos, that rolls through Paradise?
So the youth listened daily for a voice,
And sound, and teaching, words unspeakable
By mortal sage.   He watched the Morning-star
Pale in the heaven; he saw fair Êôs glide,
Rising, like Aphroditê from the sea,
But all unsensuous; her dim gleaming hands
Poured dewy waters from her pair of urns.
Then the great Sun, in amorous pursuit,

Flamed in the orient; toiled, and warred, and won,
And sank, high victim with a glorious doom,
Upon his western altar : whilst the Moon,
Walking in brightness, watched his passionate end,
And swept serene through restful realms of calm.
He marked the myriad train of Argos-eyes—
Oriôn, noted by the wary Bear,
Pleiads, and Hyads, and Boôtês slow ;
And saw some kiss the wave ; anon, return,
And aye renew their fair and featly dance.
A labour that had nought laborious ;
An energy whose happy exercise
Brightened the glad attendants of the night,
And stimulated effort; a high hymn
Pregnant with purpose dimly understood,
But felt to be all fitting and from gods ;
To breathe of worthy worship ; to imply
Melody undulating in the soul
Of earth and heaven, with vast capacity
For glorious overflowings.   These, the clouds
In endless change of form, and tint, and mass,
Unbound and wandering, like our human thoughts,
And fading off in ever-foiled attempts
To pile up airy mountains in the void,
And scale the blue ; the storm, the bow of Zeus—
All he regarded with a passionate gaze,
Which darkened as he turned again from heaven

Unsatisfied, the soul of things unsolved :
The curtain was the picture.

Then Tellis bent his searching gaze on earth,
Listened to Nature in her lowlier ways,
And strove to read her hymn. The bee that hummed
Amid the bloom, attracted his regards ;
The butterfly that flitted joyously :
The creeping-thing that knew his own abode,
And laboured by some law ; yet how and why,
Unto what end and with what slow result
Escaped him. On a rocky promontory
Facing the orient, he would love to sit,
So motionless and so enwrapped in dream
Indefinite, and yet both sad and sweet,
That all earth's lowlier children, bird and beast,
Ceased to regard his presence. The goat browsed
Close at his feet ; the sea-mew washed her wings,
And strutted by in happy vanity,
Forgetful of all fear. Then, in his soul
Spake Tellis silently : '

　　　　　　' Ye peaceful things,
That do pure service to the blessed gods
Unconsciously, or haply consciously,
Give me your calm, and take away my pain.
Yet, is it pain ? I gaze on the green earth,

And the bright heaven with rapture ; but, my joy
Melts like a northern snowflake in the sun,
Beneath the rays of a supreme desire
For a delight intenser. The ripe grape,
And all the lower cycle of delight
Beloved of man, seem somewhat base and poor ;
And but suggestive of immortal fruit,
Such as the Toiler won in the far West.
Therefore he sits at a high banquet-board ;
Crowned effort reaching to the height o' the gods,
Sphered evermore in splendour. These around
Seek nothing which they do not quickly find ;
So are they happy, aye, and innocent.
And, yet, my soul-want and unhappiness
Is sweeter than their joy. To seek, to strive
Age after age ; to see the constant stars
Return in marshalled order ; still to seek—
Oh, this were better than to find at once
A narrow happiness, though glad and pure :
Whether in sunset or in orient clime,
A golden apple or a golden fleece—
All noble souls must ever have a quest.
Yet, what seek I ? No Troia's windy towers
Allure me o'er the deep. No battle-clash
Tempts my firm sinews to a fierce delight :
No solar boat-cup by the ocean-stream
Borne to my feet, invites me o'er the main

To a bright western grove.   Can we but search
When wandering ?   Surely not.   I, motionless,
Gaze in the mirror of my human soul,
Then outward ; seeking for the golden link
That binds the gods to this daedalian world ;
And, yet, the sweet and subtle Unperceived
Escapes my spirit ; and I grope as one
Enwrapped with curious curtains in his dreams.'
Then before Tellis, as he lay and mused,
Flitted at times the damsels of the Isle—
Zênophila, Iônis, Hermonassa,
Ianthê, Hêliodôra, and the rest—
And cast on him sweet looks and more than kind.
But he, unwitting, scarcely saw them pass,
Nor noted rosy grace and snowy breast,
Light footstep, joyous laughter, and the smiles
Which gods have given to girls.   His slumbering
        soul,
Her wings unfolded and her sense inwrapt,
Viewed them, and saw them not ; and so remained
Untangled in their tresses, dark or fair.
Then the full lip was curled with some disdain
At Tellis, and the bright eye flashed contempt,
Tinged with vague bitterness for his neglect.
What seeks this dreamer with his distant gaze,
Narkissos at his fountain ?   Vain self-love
Which mars a noble presence, or a mind

Wayward, and wild, and all untunable
To the sweet music Aphroditè loves.

'Nay,' said Zênophila, 'perchance he aims
At some Kalypsô hidden in the main,
Forgetful of us poor Pênelopês,
That stay at home, and do as we are bid.
You are too sun-browned, Girls, not fair enough
For this nice Orpheus, though without a lyre.
Best leave him to the vengeance of our queen :
Hippolytos the second, lo, he seeks
The margin of the sea.   'Tis destiny ;
And old Poseidôn may produce a bull
To fright him into fragments.   Kypris knows
How to avenge our smiles on such as he,
Whilst Artemis is powerless in his cause.'

So, the fair train, half wrathful, half amused,
Trippingly in their pretty petulance,
Vanished ; and left grave Tellis to his dreams.
Then the youth turned his gaze upon the main,
Mother, and nurse, and tomb of mortal men—
And listened to the ever-rising hymn
Circling the Isle !

       ' O stormful, sorrowing Sea,
Now sullen, throbbing thunder ; now in dirge
Expression of all patience and despair ;

Now moaning in thy sleep; unto what end
Wouldst thou attain, and why dost thou lament?'

Then changed his note, exclaiming :

                      ' "Tis not grief ;
'Tis Doric music, stately, bold, and free,
Which varies to a lingering, Lydian lay,—
Soft, Seirèn singing, sweetly slow and sad.'

And, then, with sudden bitterness, he cried :

' The sea can never change : my changing moods
Of storm, of hope, of languor, or despair,
I read into its being. It knows nought,
Cares nought, feels nought, and echoes nought of
       aught ;
And, thus, my soul, entangled in herself,
Misreads the world, and takes her vagrant dreams—
Her self-reflected phantasies for truth.
And Truth is sweetest, bitter though it be ;
If we could touch her robe, although the touch
Parted the soul to Hadês, being too strong
For our humanity to grasp and live ;
Yet, even so, 'twere better than to dwell
Beneath the sway of some entangling lie.
But what is Truth ? Why muse upon the world,
Forgetful of the hour ? I may neglect

The honest purpose of a homely life,
Waiting and watching for I know not what.
Shall I descend?   Embrace the common fate?
Seek a Zênophila, and rear my brood?'

Down from the rocky promontory, Tellis
Turned with slow foot; when, suddenly, the Bird
That flies unflagging nigh the throne of Zeus,
Soared on his right; thrice circled, paused, and then
Uttered a cry; and, with aspiring wing,
Passed towards heaven, and vanished in the height.
Then, Tellis, to the nobler purpose strung,
Bent reverently his head, and prayed, and praised;
And spake, as teaching his own doubtful soul.

'See, how alone, speeds the gods' harbinger
With tireless flight, towards the lofty home,
Where, sheened in splendour the Immortals dwell.
Sail on, brave Bird!   Thy wing uplifts my heart :
Not purposeless, nor meaningless, nor vain
Spreads the bold course to shores unknown.   For He
Who scatters through the boundless universe
His starry host, the moving gems of night,
And bids them smile and shine, and beacon man
To the annual changes of an ordered world—
That Zeus, of whom his offspring stand in need,
Of whom all haunts of man are full, and full

The sounding ocean, and to whom the hymn
Unpausing rises through the echoing years;
He who with ease makes strong, and easily
Abases mortal might, brings low the great,
And with kind increase blesses the obscure;—
This self-same Power shall surely chisel out
A harmony of perfect form and thought,
Unlabouring in effort, tireless force,
Self-sphered, unending, infinite in plan;
Wherein head, heart, affections, will, and wing,
Mind's melody, Love's loveliness, and all
Which we can dream of fair and good, and more-
Shall meet, and that for ever.   'Tis a Power
Whose deathless energy will seek, and, finding,
Strike from the anvil of the earth and heaven,
The lightning sparks of splendours infinite;
Whilst a great Choir peals a triumphant hymn,
And Silence is abashed.'

So, every morning, Tellis watched the east
In patient servitude.   'I stand and wait,
Wait for a message flung from the Unseen:
And, if an impulse bids me thus to stand,
An impulse irresistible, then I
Am a faint echo of some distant truth,
Moved by its sway and flowing with its tide,
Which shall unveil her meaning and herself,

Here, now, or elsewhere in the dim To-come.
It recks not which, nor where; for, these bright
    torches,
Whose flaming motion cuts the ring of hours
From off the measureless azure, the vast soul
Of period and space enlinked in one,
Have time and times to spare. Soon, late—mere words
Whose meaning is so little or so false,
That hammers clanging on a bowl of bronze
Give out scarce less of reason.'

                     Thus he mused
And every day felt more of pure content,
And every day was more observed of men ;
His fellows of the Isle, who said : 'Some god
Enwraps his spirit; let us wait and see.'

One morn, in summer, when short-swaying Night
Hasted betimes, and sped her to her place,
Rose Tellis as she set. His eastward gaze
Saw a faint streak of silver kiss the blue ;
The star of Aphroditê paled and set,
And purer, brighter, like Athêna queen
When flashing light to Sounion, rose the dawn
In dewy robe ; behind her sped a wind,
Which with shrill voice her cloudy peplos blew,
And swept her up to heaven. Lo, from the south

A galley hasting with a bellying sail,
Mere speck upon the wave.   Tellis' keen sight
Was rivetted on it, as it grows apace,
Blown by the friendly gale.   On, on it hastes
With Zeus-sent message from the outer world;
And the youth, hearing nothing but his heart
In passionate throbbing, watched the vessel glide
Into the haven 'neath his rocky seat;
A tiny bay where played the amorous sea,
And poured caresses on the yellow sands.
As the ship beached, he hastened from his post
Towards the place, and waited with bent head,
Like one who stands a suppliant to a god.
And then there lightly stepped upon the shore
A figure all compact of gracious lines;
An undulating music, sphered in form,
Whose virginal presence, as she passed along,
Like sunbeam on a rich parterre of flowers,
Drew out from sea and shore their harmonies
And colour-splendours; till she moved enshrined
A gem in Nature's setting, and advanced,
Glowing with radiance.   The fair kosmic world
Blent with the fairer fountain of her soul
In joint outpouring; an ethereal grace
Girt her with glory, like a shining robe
And every spot seemed hallowed by her feet.

Then Tellis, gazing on her from afar,
With impulse unimagined till that hour,
Felt his blood course like flame; his brightest thought
Of possible delight in all its forms,
Higher and higher to the height of heaven,
Outdone in actual being. His dim dreams
Of what is perfect, faded like a ghost,
And all his being thrilled with glorious pain.
What meant those legends of the earlier time,
How, in the holy watches of the night,
Selênê kissed Endymiôn. Artemis
Filled her Oriôn with imperious love,
And slew him by her dart.

       'O happy fate!
And if yon virgin drew a bow at me,
How gladly would I welcome the winged death
Illumined by her smile. I do forget
My steadfastness and purpose. She is come
As herald of the gods, with high commands
In some bright message. Let me hear and wait,
And serve as time may form it.'

       Then he drew
Closer, as one who at a sacred fire
Warms his high heart to some supreme resolve,
Involving noble agony, which to escape,

Is to heroic mind intolerable,
And worse than lowest death.   Meanwhile, the Maid
Gave a brief space to prayer.   Her golden locks
Streamed like the glory of Chrysokomês,
As standing stately on the yellow sands,
She raised her eyes, spread her white arms to heaven,
And, bowing thrice to Powers unseen, exclaimed,
Whilst all the morning rang within her voice :

' Pervading father Zeus, and ye bright gods,
Heaven's conclave in the blue, I stand and raise
Glad hands of adoration, and invoke
Your blessing on my purpose and my work.
And thou, Poseidôn, of the steel-blue locks,
Zeus of the main, who linkest isle with isle,
Thanks for thy stout sea-horses' crests of foam
And tireless pace, which our endeavouring souls
Would vainly emulate.   Then, next to you,
Gods of the Island, epichorial,
My suppliant spirit turns.   Not in disdain
Or opposition to your ancient sway
Come I to Thasos; but an ambassage
Sent by the queens of Eleusinian vales,
Dêmêtêr and her Daughter; and I stand
Dêmêtêr's servitor for evermore.
So do ye now receive me, Kleobeia ;
And, lest we should offend, whate'er is meet,

By hallowed custom duly sanctified,
It shall be paid.   Then, bless me, oh, ye gods!'

                They of the Isle
Had gathered round her as she stood and praised ;
And, by her blinding beauty, and her voice
Which played upon the keys of Music's self,
Were stricken with such wonder that they knelt,
Joined in the prayer, then rose with milder eyes,
And proffered service and their country's best ;
Whilst the priest bade her welcome in the name
Of all the Isle-gods—Tyrian Héraklês,
Served by Phoinikian Thasos, who bestowed
His name upon the region ; Dionysos,
A joy to mortals from the glowing east ;
With old Seilênos and his Satyr train.

Then, after graceful thanks, said Kleobeia :

' Marvel not that I come ; I spread the light
Of Eleusinian torches in the North
Not to o'erthrow ; for, as the Morning-star
Hinders no Dawn, nor hinders Dawn the Sun,
So every measure of eternal truth
Clasps its precursor in a close embrace,
And fits with perfect and daedalian links
To the elder gifts of Time.   Not to destroy,

But to fulfil the purpose of the gods,
The expanding story of true life and love,
Braided in subtle tissues on the world,
Seen by the wise in gleams, and felt by all
In variant degree of sympathy,
I, Kleobeia, led by holy Fate,
And with white sails from Paros speeded here,
Am come to dwell amongst ye; and I stand,
Dêmêtêr's servitor for evermore.'

They of the Isle bent themselves reverently,
And cried:

   ' Hail, Kleobeia ! Be thou blest ;
And whatsoever has been laid on thee,
May wind to haven bring it.'

      But it chanced
Zênophila and her fair sisterhood
Had wandered to the shore, gazing unpleased
With curious eyes ; and when the maiden ceased,
And the throng answered, bidding her ' All hail,'
Then the bright circle of the Island maids—
A bunch of flowers whose bloom their fragrance
  marred—
Smiled each at each and pouted rosy lip,
And shot light darts, feathered with pretty scorn,
Half jest, half earnest ; for their arrows flew,

Barbed with soul-venom ; rather pain to itself
Than poisonous to others.

      ' See, she stands,
All eyes upon her, cynosure indeed !
Methinks immodest somewhat.'

       ' No, Iônis ;
For do you not perceive she is a man,
Posing as goddess ; half or quite profane
I call it ; and, whatever we may be,
We are not disproportioned, nor desire,
Like impious Giants, to reach up to heaven.'

' Step somewhat nearer. Do you mark her shoulders ?
By Aphroditê, of unequal height !
Why comes she hither ? '

      ' Doubtless her own kin
Could answer that, an they would care to tell.'

So they drew nigh, and strove to scorn, but she
Suddenly turned towards them with a smile,
And said :

    ' Fair damsels of this kindly soil,
I bow myself before you. O, the gods,
I see, remember Thasos. Happy men,
That holy earth here nurtures ! Whilst I stay,

Enrol me in your joyous sisterhood;
Give me your loves, and, Maidens, speed a Maid.'

Then, whilst they stood abashed, her mariners
From sea-chests, fastened by Sarranian cords,
Drew goodly raiment, bright with starry sheen;
Embroidered robes Sidonian skill had wrought,
The fairest for adornment; and, with these,
Necklace and earrings of the finest gold,
And gold and silver bracelets. Then she said:

'This golden lion we give Hêraklès,
The common champion of the east and west:
This kanthar to your Bakchos, who is shrined
At Delphoi with Apollôn, and who stands
With Dêô at Eleusis. Golden bee
And silver arrow are for Artemis:
Whilst I, Dêmêtêr's own Kistophoros,
Will bear her sacred chest.'

Then, with a smile,
She parted gifts amongst them; and they stood
All rosy with confusion and surprise.
So, when her gracious courtesy had lent
To each new charm from out her ample store,
And made the bevy of fair maidens shine

With added lustre, like a gem displayed
In featlier settings, she rejoiced, and said :

' There is no beauty but with beauty blends,
As truth with truth, and loving soul with soul.'

But they were tongue-tied, all abashed and sad,
Nor could find word to thank her.   Then she looked
Upon them softly, with mild, questioning gaze,
Nor further spake ; until Zênophila,
A better nature melting through sad eyes,
Advanced, and kneeling, caught her robe, and cried :

' Lady and queen, from some bright outer world,
Resume thy gifts.   The daughters of the Isle
That petulant mocked, because in their lean hearts
Rose envy of thy beauty and thy grace,
Are all unworthy.   Thou hast smitten us
With this thy biting kindness to the soul :
Pierced through the harness of our self-conceit
And shown us what we are.'

                              All bowed assent.
To whom Kleobeia, with a luminous smile,
And wave of her white hand :

                              ' O, heed not, Girls,
A breath upon the mirror of your love ;
It shows true depths to the gazer.   I perceive

Hearts full to overflowing, which, when struck,
Vibrate responsive to the noblest tones,
As Memnòn's image answers to the Sun.
I come to dwell amid your sisterhood,
A handmaid in all sweet and holy ways ;
And I, perchance, may teach you how to make
The high still higher and the fair more fair.
Ye do perceive I love you.'

                Then they all
Fell on her neck and kissed her, and were glad,
And brightened into sunshine through their tears.
Meanwhile, afar, with eye that never strayed
From Kleobeia, Tellis stood enwrapt ;
And gazed with a dim love that lost itself
In boundless reverence. An awful hope
Too vast for his humanity to bear,
Shot through his soul like lightning, and was gone,
But left him trembling ; and he felt her glance,
Which rested on him, as she gazed around,
Shake, as Poseidòn's trident shakes the earth.
Then spake the Maiden to her choir of friends :

' And who and what is yonder comely youth ?
By Loxias, 'tis a man ! Yet, statue-like,
On whom our mother Nature has enwrought,
With cunning chisel, tumult that is still.'

Then told they her of Tellis, and his life,
Lonely and silent, musing o'er the main ;
And whispered, smiling, of his disregard
Of the usual sweets of the world, the tricks of
    time ;`
But without bitterness, for in their souls
The fountains of fresh water bubbling up,
Struck from the flint by Kleobeia's touch,
Washed bitterness away. The gentler mind
Can best discern a purpose of the gods,
And so they waited, watching. Kleobeia,
Gliding in stately beauty, like a star
That touches darkness with a golden smile,
And bids it waken, moved where Tellis stood.

' Fair youth,' she cried, ' thy sisters of the Isle
Have dowered me with their love. A stranger I,
Not wandering purposeless, but hither blown
By the high mandate of all-holy Fate,
The breath that sweeps around the throne of Zeus,
Exciting infinite activities
That speed to noble goals. Hast thou no word
Of welcome for a stranger ? '

                   Tellis strove
For utterance, but his passionate heart was dumb.
Whereat the maiden marvelled, and exclaimed :

                                    E

'So noble, yet so speechless!'

                    'O my queen,'
Iônis whispered, 'thou must surely know
He is not an Ixiôn, who would dare
To clasp a goddess, but a mortal man,
Into whose vase of being thou hast poured
Draught far more potent than the Aiaian meed
Of form-destroying Kirkê.   Her fell cup
Struck human glory swineward ; thy bright gift
Might shatter such a goblet.   Have a care.'

Then Kleobeia, seeing his great love,
Unfashioned in its purpose, vague and vast,
Felt her own soul responsive ; but rejoined,
With slow sweet speech of calm serenity :

'Whether thou speak or no, I do not doubt
That thy soul answers.   Yet is mortal life,
Whate'er it may be in the time to come,
Activity and effort ; if a dream
That leads the dreamer to eternity,
Still in our dream we strive, or we should strive,
To add one note of music to the hymn
That rises from the world.   Dost know, O Youth,
The present makes the future ?   If we are fair,
Let worthy effort stamp us fairer still.
How do men call thee ?'

'Tellis,' he replied.

Then, she, slow smiling with a lingering grace,
And dainty movement of her shapely neck,
Said, 'Tellis—Telos, dost thou know the end?
Not yet, not here.   Arise and follow me.
I, Kleobeia, from Eleusinian vales,
Come to proclaim the hidden and the goal,
And broaden hope and brighten smile; to cast
Fresh sunlight o'er the shadow of the world.
And some strange power thou know'st not, may,
        perchance,
Change thee, O Tellis, into Telitês;
Not silent, but, as musical as wave
Kissed by the flying breath of the west wind.
Come, then, ye votaries in the race of life,
Toss starry torches on from hand to hand,
And speed the song, and aid me, whilst I strive,
Dêmêtêr's servitor for evermore.'

Then many moons she tarried in the Isle,
And taught Dêmêtêr's sacred mysteries;
A ritual pure, illumined with all hope.
She sang the story how the goddess Maid
In fields Nysaian playing, with her choir
Of bright-eyed nymphs, the splendours of the world.
Leukippê, rider of the snowy steed;

Phainô, apparent loveliness; Elektra,
The Beaming-one; Ianthê, violet-hued;
Sweet Melitê, Iakchê, Bakchos' mate;
The rapid grace of fair Kalliroê,
Okyroê, swift-gliding in the dance;
Golden Chryséis, and Ouraniê,
Daughter of realms on high; the tresses bright
Of Galaxurê thrown across the heavens;
And Tychê with her wheel of rolling hours;
A harmony of colour, thought, and tone,
Of rippling melody and dainty grace,
Of waving arm, and liquid eyes, whose glance
Shot innocent lightnings; suddenly was snatched
By the dark Power of sombre mightiness
Ruling in shadowed ways beneath the earth :
He plucked her brightness to illume his crypt,
Yet all in awful love : and, how the Maid,
One smile incarnate, passing through the gloom,
Developed strength and majesty supreme,
Fitted to rule and reign; to superintend
The patient purpose of slow winnowing pain;
To check the nether turbulence; to disarm
The deathless hate of inharmonious souls;
And to control the ministers whose keen sight,
Like sleuth hound, tracks the guilty.   Her white
    hand
Can stay the pitiless Fury; her firm voice

Bids Chastisement retire, its purpose past,
And whispers to the wearied soul of rest.

Then Kleobeia, traversing those keys
Of harmony, whose twisted undertones
Seem half-discordant to the shallower mind,
Sang how the awful Queen, enthroned, enringed
By all the guardian terrors of her realm,
Became the object of an impious hope—
The mad desire of two heroic souls.
These, daring all things, plunged to the abyss,
Blindly to beat their wings against her light,
And agonise before her.   Mortals take
This greediness of Beauty for true love ;
And such unhallowed, self-regarding flame
Would soil the radiant garments of the gods,
And burn heaven's lights to blackness.   Mercy's hand
Released the Athenian, but his hapless friend,
Clasped by the stony arms of the nether crag,
Sits and shall sit for ages.   Undisturbed
Flows on the even purpose of the gods ;
The queen's untrembling sceptre sways her shades,
And the eternal chorus chaunts its hymn,
Through all the murmuring cadences of pain.

Her lyre struck brighter thoughts : how every loss
Is gain of something nobler.   How the heart

That loves, must suffer somewhat ; but will make
A covenant with eternal Power, and pray
Not all unanswered.   How Persephonê
Rose from the depths at dawn by Hermês led,
Poured out her heart upon her mother's breast,
Whilst sad Dêmêtêr, brightening into bliss,
Smiled on the earth, and clad its fertile plains
With her own golden robe.   And thus the ring
Of darkness and of light, of heat and cold,
Of summer harvest and of winter snow,
Revolves harmonious.   How the buried seed,
Perchance of wheat or of some other grain,
Bursts from its prison into broader life
And smiles at heaven.   How changes of the form
Change not the subtle essence which we name
This Me, or Thee ; it springs intensified
Gladdening in nobler life.   And how the strength
Which can be now so strong, the hope so high,
The love so lovely, and the soul so fair,
Form a sure pledge and promise, sworn by Zeus,
And graven high on tablets of the heaven,
That, through all ages of the vast To-come,
The fair shall grow more fair, the pure more pure,
The true more closely kiss the lips of Truth ;
The wise more deeply drink at starry rills ;
And every hope burst into deathless bloom.
A perfect future travels to the soul :

The Beautiful that passes with the hours,
Shall in its flying transit reproduce
In endless pattern the more Beautiful,
And that for ever !

                  Then her spirit turned
To the dim past and proved her thesis there.
How from the depths of Chaos and of Night,
Rose form and order, and Titanic power
That spent itself in throes, and vanished, leaving
A calmer earth beneath the blessed sway
Of all the gods who dwell in the wide heaven.
She sang of man's first efforts ; of his quests,
And questionings, and babblings, vague and vain :
And how heroic, much-enduring souls
Wrung with slow toil its secrets from the world,
Sped east and west, and smote the sea with oars,
Rolled back the darkness, and lit dawn on dawn ;
And, clashing on the anvil of the earth,
Struck sparks of power, illumining the wise
To knowledge hidden by the deathless gods.

Then would she sing of realms beyond the sea,
And ancient heroes, whose well-labouring swords
Carved the world into kingdoms, crowned themselves,
And, diademed for ever, sit and wait
In shadowy Hadês, whilst all aftertime

Salutes their dim and silent majesty.
How, in the misty morning of the world,
Rose Babylôn in towers ; and every tower
An altar flaming to the answering stars !
How far Aigyptos, with her sacred stream,
Zeus-born in hidden springs, thought out her
    hopes,
And graved her mystic theory of the gods
On hardest granite ; energised, and built
For Cheops and for Chephrên, ancient kings,
Her temple-tombs eternal as the world.

And next she spake of Hellas, and her voice
Rose in still sweeter music, as she told
Of our dim sires, half lost in morning light ;
Of Eastern Kadmos, speeding o'er the sea
From Sarra, where the riches of the world
Sparkle and centre ; of Bellerophôn,
And how he fought ; and seemed at length to fail,
Steed-tossed, and wandering on the Aleian plain,
In melancholy exile from the gods.
Yet never can the soul heroic lose
The last prize of the contest.   Far above
Domain of Tychê and her whirling wheel,
Justice, high virgin, who has left the world,
Crowns weary brows with an immortal wreath,
Where harmony rings full.

She sang of Thebes, a shrine of lurid light,
Whose gates are sacred to the Wandering
    Stars ;
Of Oidipous, his wisdom and his woe—
And how the blind old phantom of a man,
Supported by his sweetest daughter's love,
Crawled to the grove where Night's fell children
    dwelt,
And found no Furies, but Eumenides.
At eventide was light : Zeus' thunder rolled
All sorrow to oblivion. Thêseus knelt
With shaded eyes, and saw his aged friend
Pass in strange glory to eternal peace ;
And offered adoration to the earth,
And to Olympos, seat of gods. One prayer
Included both for both are ringed by Zeus.
O conquered Darkness, where is now thy sway?
Thy victory, Pain, is ended. The tried soul
War-worn with many conflicts, lays aside
The battered harness and the broken sword,
And rests for ever. A succeeding race
Untutored by experience, still produce
Fresh passion-nurtured pangs. The battle-storm
Thundered anew in Kleobeia's strain ;
When the fierce Seven, with dread emblazoned
    shields,
Dashed to the onset, and the Brothers died

In undivided hatred; their sad race
Wind-drifted downward to Kôkytos' wave.

Of the stern fortune which attends the Good
Entangled with the Evil, next she sang.
Amphiarâos, destined to the grave,
Foreknowing his own ruin, yet compelled
By Fate to dare the hopeless, and consort
With god-defying men.   Yet, even here,
Heaven doth not leave its votaries.   Father Zeus
Clove the deep-bosomed earth with burning bolt,
And hid the hero, and his flying steeds
Secured for ever; whilst his deathless voice,
Oracular, still echoes from the shrine
Which man, and beast, and bird alike revere.

And, then, in low sweet music, she proclaimed
The story of Antigonê; her love
For sire, for brother, stronger far than death
And lawless law, and all the general voice
That twitters feebly on the tyrant's side.
How the fair maid, with bitter wail like bird
Lamenting its robbed nest and vanished brood—
Drew with white hands and all unused to toil,
The clammy Polyneikês, stark and cold;
Gave him to holy earth, and from the urn
Thrice with libations crowned the luckless dead;

Defiance to an edict not of Zeus,
Or Justice, dweller in the height and depth.
How, dragged before the judgment seat, she dared
The utmost fury of the perishing slave
Who thought by proclamation to repeal
Those laws of the Immortals which remain
Unwritten and immovable; not now,
Nor yesterday, but endlessly they live,
Originating in a dateless past,
Beyond the flight of thought.   How, led to death,
In swanlike dirges she outpoured her soul—
As bride of Acheron, unblessed, unloved,
With ears that never heard the marriage lay,
Husbandless, childless, left by fawning friends,
Her bridal chamber an unhallowed tomb—
And yet through all, unshaken, firm as Fate,
Deeming the Dwellers underneath the earth
Not hostile to her cause : that Mother, Sire,
And Brother could regard her still as dear ;
Whilst those great Powers who marshal mortal shades,
Would meet her with absolving eyes, and give
Eternal welcome, wondrous strange and sweet.

She paused, and then continued : ' Love is first,
Unconquered in the fight, couched in the cheek
Of youthful maiden,'—here Iónis smiled—
' Roamer beyond all seas : nor high, nor low,

Escape his sceptre. E'en the blessed gods
Are mystically lovers ; but, O Power,
Bestowing pain so glorious, purge my soul ;
Nor turn it on the common sweets of time,
Which burn themselves to ashes. No disdain
Of the vast impulse of our happy youth,
Be mine, be yours : no scoff at kiss or clasp ;
Pandêmôs may be holy. Yet upraise
Your true affections past these mortal ties,
And see Ouraniè gleaming through the stars,
Unspeakable in loveliness ; espy
Eternal Beauty waiting to embrace
A soul that shall be ever young as she.
And they who grasp this guerdon, will not grieve
If, missing Kypris, they should find our earth
Cold ante-chamber of a glowing shrine.'

And then her voice rose like a trumpet blast,
Recalling Ilion—all its war and wail ;
The mighty Agamemnôn, king of men,
The vainly-striving Hectôr and his foe,
A battle-storm incarnate ; with their trains
Achaian, Troian, roaring as the sea.
And, then she spake of labouring Hêraklês,
Hight Monoöikos,* of the lonely house,

* Whence the modern ' Monaco.'

Which first he built to Hêlios in the West,
When sailing in the golden cup o' the Sun,
He dared the world's far edge, found light and
    shade ;
Persephonê's own poplars, and the shores
Of dim Kimmeria. ' Yet even there
Is Leukê, where Achilleus dwells in light ;
And that immortal fruit which Hêraklês
Plucked from the jaws of Terror. Do we serve
Eurystheus? 'Tis but seeming; we serve Zeus.
The petty tyrant passes. The great will
That dowers us with this noble servitude,
Without which prize were valueless, flows on
In broader, brighter volume, and we win.
The choric dance, wherein all Nature joins,
Both starry ether, and the forms that float
Aërial, oceanic, or of earth,
A sacrifice and never-ending rite,
Wheels round the world with many twinkling feet,
In ordered strophe and antistrophe.
And those who hear the vast, innumerous tread,
Are filled with fire, and shaken to the soul,
As Dionysos shakes his native Thebes.
And, yet, this rhythmic movement infinite,
This glowing circle, this immense desire,
Throbs to one central purpose, seeks one goal,
Bathes in the crystal fountains of one will,

Sings but one song in ever variant tones,
Lights myriad torches to illume one truth,
And lives eterne for One.   Then, through the
    dance,
In all its mazy windings, fast and far,
Or sphered in splendour with the Aithiop queen,
Or shadowed by the ways beneath the earth,
Lead Kleobeia, Zeus and holy Fate.'

So many moons she tarried in the Isle,
And crept into all hearts.   The common folk,
Who spent laborious days, and, toiling, reaped
The harvest of the sea, or from the earth
With patient hand drew simple livelihood,
Beheld her as a goddess.   Aged priests,
Soul-hardened by the custom of their creed
Into slack service and mechanical,
Mere urns for holding ashes of the dead—
Regained lost heights, and felt the sacred fire
Rekindle in their hearts.   For the great gods
Who hide themselves have lent us those they love,
To stimulate the earthward-turning mind,
Unworthy impulse, and our low regards.
Therefore a sweet and starry chain of souls,
Diviner texture, dawns upon the world ;
And, wound around the common clay of man,
Raises from sleep material, retransforms ;

Then, startling him with his unconscious strength,
A possibility of infinite good—
Lifts him towards the gods.   The children crept
On Kleobeia's knee, and stroked her locks,
And, with keen sense of beauty, murmured, ' Oh ! '
For, they who dower the tiny hand with might,
To make it Love's own sceptre, have endowed
The little heart with skill intuitive
To recognise the Good.   As one who knows
The sculptor's art perceives, amid a mass
Of carven failures which perpetuate
The common undertype, a chiselled thought,
Fragment of form divine, and instantly,
Joys in its power ; so, little guileless ones
That have not known world-baseness, recognise
Heaven's masterpieces, both of body and soul ;
And chirp and twitter, like a bird in spring,
Babbling their blessings.   Overflowing love,
Whate'er it suffer, meets an answering stream,
And both rejoice together.   Thus the Maid
Lived perfumed life.   The Manhood of the Isle
Had died for one sweet look.   The damsels saw
Themselves in Kleobeia glorified,
Their stature heightened, their true womanhood
Zoned with a sacred splendour ; like a shrine,
Which sparkles at the presence of a god.
While the warm loves that played across their souls,

Beamed from their eyes, and dimpled rosy cheek,
Were touched with something holier, and became
That composite of earth and starry heaven,
So high, and yet so human, which we hold
True mortal goddess of our vast desires,
Pandêmos, yet Ouraniê evermore.

Thus reigned and ruled Dêmêter's servitor :
But, whilst she gathered sweetness from all
    hearts,
Each rosy nymph that sways the flying hours,
In passing, shook into the Maiden's soul,
A drop of dew from Kypris' myrtle branch,
And all for Tellis. At the first she smiled,
Deeming these touches sparks of wandering fire
Thrown by the hand of tricksy little Loves,
Harmless as summer lightning. Still, she saw
With ever more of interest, how the Youth,
In reverence and noble self-restraint,
Virtue and valour, was indeed a man
Worthy a heart's devotion. Such a soul,
So grandly shrined, so tender, yet so strong,
Might circle woman's weakness, aid her strength,
Support her footsteps on the rugged path
That leads to the seat of the gods. And then she
    frowned
In scorn of her own tenderness.

Can I,
I, Kleobeia, Dêô's votary,
Self-sphered within my service ; and myself
Raised, like the Pythia, from the crowd of maids
Whose fate and whose ambition is to serve
As wives for men, bear children, live and die—
Can I descend from these keen mountain heights
Nearer the gods, and nearer to that light
Which heaven reflects in some pellucid souls
Unstirred by earthly passion? Can I yield
To Aphroditè? Rather let me pass,
Like Pallas, Shaker of the shafts of light,
Unclaimed by Eros, to eternal Zeus.'

But, whilst her soul spoke bravely to itself,
Smiled at the touch of Kypris, scorned her sway,
Planned a bold flight with solitary wing—
Love's sweet, soft, baby fingers touched her heart,
And that was lost for ever. As the Dawn,
All cold, and clear, and virginal, uplifts
Calm eyes to heaven, yet, whilst she seems alone,
Is thrilling at the rising of the Sun ;
Changes her colour, throbs in rosy red,
And then, o'ermastered by his burning gaze,
Sinks in his arms and dies in ecstasy—
So Kleobeia, o'ercome by that great pain,
Devoid of which the splendour of our life

F

Is poor indeed, like flower surcharged with dew,
Bent her fair head, and murmured, 'Gods, I love.'

At length, her work accomplished, came the day
When she must leave the Island; seek the shrine
Of Eleusinian Dêô, and report
Her purpose ended with supreme success.
The fateful morning dawned; the barque was
    there,
Ready with oar and sail; a favouring wind,
Offspring and gentle breath of the wide heaven,
Beckoned the Maiden southward to her goal :
And Kleobeia stood beside the sea,
Visible sunlight, undulating grace,
Awful in very sweetness, a bright link
Which joins the tear-stained record of mankind,
And binds its weakness and infirmity
To the very throne of Zeus.   For these great souls
That reach heroic stature, live and breathe
The ordered strophe and antistrophe
Of the choric song of Time; o'erpower the woe,
Beat down the inharmonious, scatter hope
Like golden drops of sunlight; and tears cease,
And earthly wailing fades in melody.

Around her mourned the Isle.   'Oh, stay,' they cried,
'Light, Healing, Helper, Virgin, half divine!'

'Stay with us,' said the Priest; 'illume our shrines,
And bring us nearer to the blessed gods.'

'Stay with us,' wailed the Old; 'support our steps,
And tell us of that realm beyond the stream,
Guiding us to the boat.'

               With agonised hearts,
'Stay with us,' groaned the Youths; and children
    plucked
At Kleobeia's robe with tiny hands,
And wept and prayed her, full of sweet, strange
    power,
Which is their gift from heaven, not to forsake
The little ones of the Isle who loved her so.
Then Kleobeia felt her passionate heart
Throb wildly, 'neath the rush of sympathy,
And tremble at the shock of human love
Outpoured in all profusion. But her soul,
Conscious, though dimly, of another fate,
Serenely true, drove backward gathering tears;
And calm, and sweet, and steady rose her voice,
Amid a silence sad as Niobè's :

'O Thasians, who have loved me, whom I love,
Who have received me as a messenger
From Zeus and from Dèmètèr, never mourn

The destiny of any.   My glad toil
Here in your Isle, a joyous sacrifice,
Is over and for ever.   Ye possess
The sacred ritual, with its deathless hopes
Of infinite advance.   These gliding years,
That pluck our mortal beauty piece by piece,
With silent, subtle, and remorseless hands,
Add to the spirit every charm they strip
From its poor vesture, which we prize so much :
And, when their task is over, and the Soul,
A harmony of splendour, stands complete
In raiment worthy undecaying spheres,
They gently lead her thither.   As for me,
I go to the appointed.   Do not grieve :
Remember that I loved you ; for your love
Is as a necklet twined around my soul,
And resting on my heart.   I do not think
Again on earth to see your kindly smiles ;
But, if we meet in that supernal world,
To which all sweetness tends, we shall be glad
As Love itself can make us.'

                              Here she paused :
And Tellis, who was standing in the throng,
With downcast eyes, and silent as a grave,
Felt his soul darken.   Suddenly there flashed
O'er the low brow of the hill, in gliding form

Of ordered strophe and antistrophe,
The maidens of the Isle—one sacred dance,
A noble Diplê, joyous but serene ;
From east to west in circling gracefulness,
Swept the fair forms and sped the rapid feet—
Theonoê, Ereuthô, Rhodokleia,
Ianthê, Hermonassa, Hêliodôra,
Zênophila, Iônis, and the rest—
And then from west to east, as the brave Sun
Ploughs through the Under-world, Oriòn-like,
And seeks the eastern wave to gain and give
Fresh sight to earth and heaven.   Still, as they
        danced,
Melodious ever rose the choric song,
Praising Apollôn and his Artemis,
And Hêra, who the keys of marriage keeps,
And Hermês, and the gods and Nymphs of the Isle,
And last the great Dèmêtèr.   Kleobeia
Smiled with delight to see them look so fair,
Brighter by their bright service ; the sad crowd
Parted before them, and the radiant band
Glided to where the gracious Maiden stood,
And halted in her presence ; whilst their chief,
Zênophila, the leader of the train,
Bent her fair head before Dèmêtèr's Maid,
And knelt as to a goddess.   Raising then
Her dewy eyes towards the beautiful face :

' Lady and Queen,' she murmured, ' ere you go,
The daughters of the Isle, whom you have dowered
Not merely from your store, but, oh, far more
From your great hive of sweetness, lacking which
How poor are mortal charms—pour out their hearts
Before the shrine of your supremest grace ;
And tell, as best we can, by these our tears,
How much we owe you, and how much we love.
For you have raised our feebler womanhood,
Taught us our stature, bid us stand upright.
Seen in the mirror of your glorious soul
And high revealings, we behold ourselves
Not merely children, playing with the world,
Nor yet the petted playthings of a man ;
But maids whose duty and whose privilege
It is to join the choric dance of Time
With sires, and brothers, and still sweeter mates ;
Work out a noble purpose, hand in hand,
Supply those strains of music which men lack,
Till harmony rings full ; and, when the time
Is ripe for Aphroditê, and the Queen
Who sits by Zeus pours blessing, change from maids
To matrons ; mothers of a noble race,
Worthy our Hellas' love.   So, when we fade,
And pass into the shadow, no regret
For wasted purpose in the time gone by
May mar our ending.   Thus we trust to stand

The not unworthy compeers of a man,
As Artemis by Apollôn, Hêra by Zeus,
And this we owe to thee.　Therefore, O Queen,
As we are but poor maids of a distant Isle,
Far from those centres where Hellenic life
Throbs fullest, and has grander utterance,
Accept this tribute of our love ; and think
If we had aught more beautiful and fair,
It should be yours.'

　　　　　　She ceased ; the sisterhood
Murmured their sorrowing chorus of assent :
Then Kleobeia kissed them, and they wept.
There was a pause, whilst every heart stood still,
And Kleobeia, through all her stately strength
In settled purpose, a supreme resolve
Upheld by high belief that Fate is well,
And triumph certain in the years to come—
Beside the pang of parting from the Isle,
Felt something vague and vast tug at her heart ;
Till all her womanhood trembled, and her voice
Died into silence.　Then, Zênophila,
Doubtless some god inspiring, slipt away,
Glided where Tellis stood, and took his hand,
And led him forward, moving as in dream ;
Like some most stately captive barbarous men
Are offering to Taurika ; so he

Passed through the folk to Artemis indeed.
And, thus, whilst Kleobeia, one mute surprise
In wide-eyed beauty, like the Samian queen,
Stood motionless, the quick Zênophila
Laid Tellis' hand in hers, whilst all the crowd
With one vast heart of honest human love,
Broke forth in a great shout ; yet found their joy
Commingled strangely with a burst of tears.
Then said Zênophila, and as she spake,
Bewitching Kypris echoed in her voice,
And dimpled in her smile !

                  ' Though poor, O Queen,
Thine handmaids can bestow a worthy gift ;
A worshipper whose vast and silent love
Perchance might move a goddess. It may be
The dreaming Tellis still has scorned us Girls ;
Yet we forgive him, knowing well the cause ;
No traitor he to Kypris, though he seem.
Therefore, as still the good must seek the good,
Beauty to beauty, and to dawn the sun,
Take thou our Tellis : first fruits of the Isle,
Thy servitor, and Dêô's, evermore ! '

She ceased, and all the throng thundered applause :
Then Kleobeia, through whose passionate heart
And swift intelligence, a storm of thought,

Whose rush was half the fulness of a life,
Had swept as in an instant—her fair face
One glory of the rose—renerved her soul
With a vast effort, shook herself to calm,
And, smiling with Olympian majesty,
Still holding Tellis' hand.

                  'O noble Youth,
Thy country's grace and strength personified,
An offering worthy of a king to the gods,
Art thou content to leave these Thasian shores,
That bright-eyed choir of beauty, thine old home,
And all the memories of love which cling
About the spot where first heaven's holy light
Dawned on our eyelids, climb the perilous wave,
Taking such chance as Time and Fate may bring?'

And Tellis answered with his steadfast eyes,
Earnest beyond all tears, and lit with light
From vaster possibilities of joy
Than earth's poor smiling. Then he bent his head.
And Kleobeia, who grasped that full assent,
Beholding in it purpose and resolve
Beyond all time-shocks, pointed to the ship,
Waved him on board, and, turning to the Girls,
Again she kissed them, and again they wept,
Sorrowing that they should see her face no more.

So now, all farewells ended, Kleobeia
Stretched her white hands in blessing from the deck;
Then, as the stout oars smote the summer sea,
And Boreas, quickly speeding to the south,
Eager for Oreithyia, drave them fast,
Vanished the splendours of her gracious form,
Passed to the unapparent; as the star
Of Aphroditê pales in morning heaven.

Soul-desolate and gazing o'er the sea,
Yet felt they, through the bitterness of Time,
A dew of holy influence, pure gift
Best unguent for the heart.   The mournful crowd
Departed slowly; last, the choir of Maids,
Each with the memory of Kleobeia
As jewel round her neck, resought their homes
With sweet uplifted purpose, statelier tread,
And the great knowledge, born of holy fear,
That, where the gods have placed us, we should stand
And do our service; seeing service true
Is done within a shrine, and links itself
To that eternal splendour of all good
Which dominates the world.   So passed they thence;
Blessing to others, they were blessed themselves:
And still the Thasians tell of Kleobeia.

Meanwhile, swift speeding, like the circling hawk,

Her bold barque cleft the main ; the curling wave
Of the ungarnered, deeply-flowing sea
Rushed mightily behind.   The white sails stretched,
Filled with the breath of heaven, a wafting wind,
Glided along the sea-path ; and the oars
Orderly smote the water, till the grey wave
Seethed as the strong blades tossed it.   Thus they
    sped ;
Far on the left Saôkê soared to heaven ;
And rugged Samos, where the Mighty dwell,
Frowned on them, guardian of a cult unknown ;
Whilst giant Athos, mount of Zeus divine,
Loomed on the right, seen dimly through a haze—
The veiling garment of the Nymphs of light—
Lampetiê, clad in long and flowing robe,
And Phaëthousa with her tresses fair.
Fast speeds the barque by Lemnos' smoking isle,
Where fell Héphaistos as a flame from heaven,
Rekindling earth in answer : and the hours
Glided towards the chambers of the West ;
And the sun set, and all the watery ways
Were darkened, and the Thrakian sea was passed.

Then the fair chorus of the nightly stars,
Bright potentates that seasons bear to men,
Flamed from the unapparent.   Sank the wind
To softer whisper, and the oars were still ;

Whilst all the gods that high Olympos hold
Shed sleep upon the eyelids of the crew,
Saving the helmsman. Unsupported heaven,
The peplos of Harmonia, glowed with eyes
In Argos splendour. Kleobeia's soul
Soared through the ether to the lofty home
Whence Seirios and Oriôn dart their rays,
Noting how Night divine, expanded Night,
Night, daughter of the sky, who starts from heaven,
Gazes on many places, fills all space,
And darkness fights with lustre. Gravely glad
She, 'mid the solemn stillness, standing mute,
Gazed on the starry labyrinth ; and mused
If these encircling ever-burning lamps,
In pattern, or, to mortals, patternless,
Were seen enigma, aspect kosmical,
Of the eternal, all-pervading mind,
Root, summit, first, and latest of the gods ;
Whose operations, lost in shadowy heights
And depths abysmal, sparkle down the years
In order with a strange disorder linked,
Or so it seems to man. Her gladness waned,
And something of confusion and of doubt
Stole darkly through her soul ; when, turning round,
She saw, with sweet confusion, at her side,
The stately Tellis standing; heard his voice,
And listened, as we listen to the tones

Of one who speaks in a melodious dream
Which it were death to wake from.

                        ' Kleobeia !
Divinest of earth's daughters, whom my soul
Has mirrored and has imaged from the day
When first heaven's light was fair to me ; whom I
Have seen in fugitive dreams, whose beautiful form
Is Êôs risen on noon, beacon and goal,
Star Priestess of eternal melody !
Although thou standest, ringed with sacred light,
So fair, so pure, so distant from the world—
Yet even I, the Isle's unworthy gift,
Borne in thy barque, and linked in fate with thee,
Am bold through my great love, which dares to die
If need be, or to live, or any path
Which any mortal or immortal Power
Can portion me—to say I love thee, Sweet :
And I will love thee through all time. My star,
Upon the stars thou gazest : would I were heaven
To gaze on thee with all his myriad eyes !'

He paused, and at the passion of his soul
The Maiden trembled ; then stood statue-like
As Daphnê 'neath Apollôn's burning love.
Whilst Tellis, like a noble stream that bursts
All obstacles, and rushes to its goal,

Naught heeding, hurrying in impetuous might,
Flowed on with force resistless.

                                    ' Kleobeia,
Thy greatness lifts me to the height o' the gods !
My like-unlike, my glorious Oversoul !
Whose sweet resembling difference clasps my heart
Subtly to thine, so rounds a perfect arc,
And adds to all the music of the world
Its choicest theme.   Ah, how thy soft hand thrills !
Let me but win thy love ; for, as thy smile
Cannot descend on one unworthy, I,
If thou wilt love me, shall win all with thee,
Who art my hopes personified.   With thee
Comes every perfect gift ; the bloom of Time,
The starry possibilities beyond,
And all of sweetness hid in lap of heaven ;
Eternal light, and stateliest Truth, advance
Past mortal goals, passage of human greatness
To a diviner stature.   Do I dare
Beyond all daring, hope beyond all hope ?
The venture is too great for fear.   Thy love
Sweeter than life, more precious than the spoils
Brought from the orient by Kêtaian men,
It must be mine !   But, if I have it not,
Ingloriously I will not live.   May Fate
Summon the deathful spirits of the storm,

And blast me into chaos ! Speak, my Sweet,
Tell me I live, and link my soul with thine.'

And Kleobeia—she who knew so much,
Spake so profoundly, garnered up the past,
Queened it within the present, faced the Fates,
Mantled in robe of knowledge and of grace—
Found not a word to utter ; bent her head,
Clasped her white arms around his stately neck,
And answered with a burst of happy tears.

Then Tellis, drawing her beauty to himself,
And terror-shaken with excess of joy,
Murmured :

      ' My Child, my Goddess, Kleobeia !
Do not so much as whisper. I am glad
Beyond all utterance. If I die to-night
I shall have touched an agony of joy
Which links me with Immortals.'

            Then their lips,
Their souls upon them, met ; and holy Night
Smiled from the zenith, the divine of heaven,
To see such love as this. O sacred hour,
When human heart speaks out to human heart,
Whilst the sweet wonder of our mortal love,

So fair, so fragile, so enwrapped with tears,
Is echoed by a sweeter voice divine,
Promising auguster heights, and ultimate
Enthronement 'mid the ever-circling choir.
Then sped in silence a long, rapturous pause,
A coming, an Eleusis of the end :
The night wheeled high, and star and planet passed
On spotless paths accustomed.   Kleobeia
Gently displacing his most gentle arm,
Rose to her height, and flashing towards heaven
Splendour of radiant eyes, the home of hope,
With grave, sweet utterance, raised her lyre and
    sang :

' Sing Kleobeia !   For holy Night on high,
    The blessed Night that doth to gods belong—
Sits crowned and throned in starry majesty ;
    And the full tide of Being, sweet and strong,
    Welling from depths of everlasting song,
Pours clearer utterance, now that day is done,
Rich with the dying love of the expiring Sun.

' Sing Kleobeia !   The fragrance of the world
    Is wafted to the vault ; and the deep blue,
As speeds our barque with flying sail unfurled,
    Stoops to embrace the sea's cerulean hue :
    Noon's fleeting phantoms, faded from the view,

Leave the rapt soul to spread her folded wings,
And move towards the height of heaven's mysterious
  things.

'Thy voice shall join the never-tiring choir,
  Which rolls throughout all space, towards the
    shrine
Where Being's sentient source, ethereal fire
  Exults in cloudless energy divine ;
    And, showering on our nature infantine,
Gifts worthy love, unfolds the patient plan
By which to reach the goal of stately-statured man.

' Sweet echoes call us from a distant place,
  And spur us on to greet them : we behold
The flying Perfect, laughing at our chase,
  With words unspoken and with thoughts untold ;
    No mortal vase her burning wine can hold :
And, then, we pause with faint and trembling gaze,
That seeks yet shrinks at sight of unfrequented
  ways.

' The starry Lyre is strung to greet mine own :
  I shall not sing unanswered, heaven is kind ;
Fear not, nor sink to querulous undertone ;
  Faint not, but seek, and seeking, thou shalt find
    The veiled truth.   Eternal Mind to mind

G

Dim oracles revealing through all Time,
Which bid unceasing hope untiringly to climb.

' What we are now is nothing : we shall be
    A music and a memory of delight,
Passed through all portals, and allowed to see
    Diviner splendours of the Infinite;
    Spirits eterne, in featly raiment dight ;
For, as Zeus liveth, nought shall ever roll
Twixt Kleobeia's love and Tellis' godlike soul

' Sing Kleobeia!   The moon must wane and pass :
    Stars pale from heaven, friends leave us, suns
        depart ;
Yet, when we fly, as shadow from the grass—
    Still shall I know, my Tellis, that thou art
    Unchanged in changing : and thy glorious heart
Is Kleobeia's for ever !   Thou and I,
Linked in immortal chain with heaven's high har-
    mony ! '

So, all too quickly the love-dropping hours—
Soft, shadowy sheen, with silvery sweetnesses
Above, beyond the pleasure of the last—
Sped to their place appointed.   In the east
An impress faint of the undying light
Paled Darkness' robe ; and she, with all her train

Of adamants, drew back to furthest heaven ;
Fair Êôs, rising, filled her dewy urns,
Whilst Phôspheros returned her smile and died.
Faster the barque speeds on ; from out the wave
Apollón's fish in joyous circles leaps ;
As when the Master of all light and rhythm
First led his friends to Pythô. Thus they sailed
Past Skyros, where the bones of Thêscus rest,
And where Achilleus dwelt amid the maids,
Until they sighted Andros, noted seat
Of the fair Wine-god, who, from Baktrian walls
Stormed westward in unconquerable might,
More pitiless than Arès, and enshrined
His worship in Kadmeian portals seven.
So swept they round Euboia with favouring wind,
Beheld the circlers of the sacred Isle,
Touched fertile Keôs, rounded Sounion's steep,
And headed for Aigina, whose great king
Corruptless, with his copesmates rules below.
Then, as they drew to holy Salamis,
Spake Kleobeia :

       'The annual time is nigh
When at Eleusis, her high sanctuary,
Fair-chapleted Dêmêtêr, holding state,
Reveals to favoured men, and gives to See.
Thou must behold, as I beheld, that both

With knowledge equal and with equal eyes,
May stand together, meet the dim To-come,
And tread towards the gods. The steadfast soul
Should feel no fear of progress dark or bright,
Or chthonian, or supernal. Dêô's rites
Are more than other rituals, as the gods
Are greater than the heroes. At the end
When thou hast passed all portals, and hast seen,
I will await thee on the terrace steps
That front the orient ; and, dear Love, may those
Immortal watchers over mortal men,
Who noiseless sweep o'er many-nurturing earth,
And scan just judgments and unholy acts,
Protect thee to the goal. When we are one
In knowledge and in faith, and time has filled
The waxing crescent, then—if these poor charms—
For body is a suffering of the soul,
Fate, burden of necessity, and chain—
Attract thee, Tellis, as perchance they may—
Since heaven has made me fair, they shall be
        thine ;
The chaste Dêmêtêr's priestess can attest
Our plighted faith. I doubt not thine will stand ;
And Kleobeia shall bow before her lord.
Nay, do not vow, I trust thee to the end.
We soon shall reach Phalêron ; when you land
Pray in Dêmêtêr's temple ; leave me there.

I shall not see thee till the holy night
When thou hast passed the portals.'

       Then the Youth
Bent his bright head, and answered :

         ' Be it so.
Thy soul is with me wheresoe'er I am ;
And, when the goddess has revealed her lore,
And I have passed the portals, I will haste
To meet my goddess on the terrace steps.

So the swift ship, her prosperous course fulfilled,
Entered Phalêron, where the lovers prayed,
Silent in Dêô's shrine. Then Tellis left,
Obedient to the word of Kleobeia,
And sought Eleusis as Elysion.

The Thasian, his probation passed, and all
The threshold ceremonial ended, stood
Without the Telestêrion, as alone,
Enringed with holy Night. Fear not, ye Powers,
Who touch the humble of the human race
With healing edges of your starry robes,
Dmêteira, Korê, and the luminous train
Of incense-fraught Eleusis, sceptred Queens—
Fear not that I should raise, with hand profane,

The veil upon your splendours. Zeus-sent dreams
Restrain the tongue, and sacred silence reigns.
What may be told of mystic rites we learn
From Samian Arignôtê, whom the mild
Azêsia honours as a Kleobeia,
Interpreter of light. The double torch
Beckons approach ; the softly-rising hymn
Breathes heavenly harmony, and the poor world
Of outer sense and stuff material fades ;
Whilst the true soul, whose finer instincts rise
Through the external up towards the seat
Of blessed Potencies, beholds their sphere
In one swift span from past to future. This,
Pregnant with promise of diviner days
In brightening undulation. Yet he sees
Not actual reality, but the True,
The poem of existence, the high will
Of all-controlling, vast Benevolence,
In a dream aspect ; partly born of earth,
And partly borrowed from the realm beyond,
Whence flash the apparitions of the gods,
And come these subtle utterances, high words
In meaning manifold, deep logogriphs,
Which He who wears the purple diadem,
And the supremest wreath of myrtle, scatters
Amid the light and glory of the scene.
Then, as the darkness died, and golden beams,

Breathing of perfume, showed the mystic realm,
The drama flowed through all its sheeny links,
That flash forth Nature; Nature, as it joins
With the high gods; for all the mysteries
Have one intent—to knit us with the True;
Which, being as it is, is free from change,
Yet grandly changing to the broader mind
From splendour unto splendour. He who sees
The outward show, perceives to such extent
As his own likeness unto loveliness
Is strong to aid him; for true vision lies
In real similarity betwixt
Perceiver and perceived. So the pure soul
Of Tellis drank with an immortal thirst
For highest beauty, at these sparkling springs;
He pierced the luminous shadows, saw the Maid'
Playing in Nysa, 'mid her gleaming choir,
Snatched to abysmal depths, to reappear
In splendour unapproachable; the quest—
Dark-robed Achaia wandering o'er the earth.
Lifting in vain the ever-blazing torch,
Until she paused beneath the stately home
Of Eleusinian Kelios; saw the Queens
In reunited ecstasy of love;
The Mother press to her immortal heart
Her blossom of a Daughter, and high peace
Reign betwixt god and god; then saw the cult

Taught by the goddess to the men of old—
Eumolpos' might, horse-pricking Dioklês,
Triptolemos, the law-delivering king—
Whilst all the happy earth, weighed down with flowers,
Laughed in the sunshine, waved her golden hair,
And sang Dêmêtèr's praises.   Blest is he
Of mortals who beholds the glorious truth :
A better fortune waits him 'neath the gloom ;
With open eyes he sees, and he attains.
The dog-shaped furies of terrestrial life
Pass into nothing, and the sleep of sense
Is lost in high awakenings.

　　　　　　　　　Night rode high
When Tellis, all the portals past, and all
The ritual ended, dowered in soul with light,
One smile incarnate, sought the terrace steps
That front the orient.   Did Pêrephoneia
Await his coming ?   Surely one as fair.
Korê Sôteira's self she seemed ; her brows
Bore diadem that flashed with starry light
Upon the sacred corn-wreath ; pendent gems
In either shapely ear, gave answering gleams
To lustre from a necklace, such as graced
Harmonia's charms in Thebes.   Her luminous eyes
Shot summer lightnings through a flowing veil
Diaphanously delicate ; her white robes

Shrouded a shrine indeed, the gate o' the gods,
The portal of all ecstasy, fair and pure
As the blue firmament, whose spotless sheen
Conceals divinest splendours ; whilst her voice,
Rich with the music wafted us in dreams
From regions with more melody, sighed :

                              'Come,
O come, Beloved ! I await thee here,
My Lord and King, my Partner and mine Own
In knowledge and in faith. My utmost soul
Is thine in holy love, as thou art mine ;
And, when to-morrow's sun shall kiss the wave,
We two will stand together, thou and I,
Before Dêmêtêr's priestess, clasp our hands,
For *Marriage is the end*, and, with one soul,
Tread upwards to the gods. On this fair night,
Whilst the bright brotherhood of starry heaven
Smile on us from the vault, and the warm breath
Of the sweet, dying wind enwraps us, we—
A maiden and her lover—will be glad
In happy vigil never known before,
And never to return. I do not doubt
Of all the love and loveliness to come ;
But this one phase, this instant of our lives
Pure in its passion as can be the kiss
Of brother and of sister, yet a love

Transcending theirs, as heaven is more than earth,
It is so sweet, my Tellis, I could kneel
And thank Eternal Goodness, with a heart
Stilled by intensest feeling into calm
More powerful than most passionate utterance
That ever burst from soul.'

　　　　　　　　　　To whom the Youth,
Tremulous with his weight of happiness,
Murmured :

　　　　　　' If all the flaming wheels of Time
Stopped, and for ever, on this sacred night,
And made it an eternity ; the stars
Burning for aye above us, and thine eyes
Answering to all the tumult of my soul,
Tellis were well content.　'Twere heaven enough,
My Bride, for me.'

　　　　　　　　　He took the soft, white hand,
And drew her beauty to him ; she upturned
Her yielding loveliness, and their two souls
Kissed like Immortals, then were still as death ;
Whilst those eternal beacons in the blue,
Love-lighted, lighted love.

Then, Kleobeia, playing with his hair,
Which blent with her own tresses :

'See, mine Own,
Yon starry labyrinth, serene and high,
Whose gleaming mantle veils divinest Truth ;
From times Ogygian glowing still the same.
What is the pattern of immortal Mind
Which runs throughout its tissues?   Are there
    depths
Far in the azure, eye has never seen?
Infinite maze of beauty !   I aspire
To taste the chalice of that deathless life
That feeds thine energy.   O flying Time,
Marked by the transit of yon flaming worlds !
O space, the temple of eternal God,
The soul of Kleobeia bids ye hail !
For I, and Love, and Tellis, we are one,
And lift one soul towards you ; whilst ye smile
Serenest benison, as on a shade
Led by our Hermès from the right hand o' the pyre
To Rhadamanthys !   Aye, and all things flow ;
The stormful, mortal race across the earth
Bursts passage, conquers, and is lost to sight
In sometime darkness : yet behind, beyond,
High Truth and Justice, Victory and Love,
Sit crowned and throned !   O hidden world of light,
Whose dimmest jewels, flung to mortal ken,
Shine like Arcturus yonder, we are thine !
Thy votaries and aspirants we burn,

And, when our mortal mantles fade and fall,
Receive thy Children ! '

        Tellis whispered : ' Pray,
My glorious Priestess, pray that holy Love,
As he has led us hither, step by step,
From far Odônis ; joined our hearts and lives
For some fair purpose, veiled in kindly light,
May grant us of his sweetest and his best,
Through all the blossoming years.'

Then Kleobeia : ' Give us of Thy best ! '

' Yea, of Thy best,' said Tellis.

        One white arm
Was stretched towards the majesty of heaven,
Her other hand was locked in his ; her face
Fixed on the dwelling of the blessed gods,
Far above storm, and care, and canker, and the loss
Which we call change, was radiant with a hope
That raised her beauty to such loveliness
As cannot rest on earth. The temple-star
Ascendant in the orient's midnight blue,
Blazed on them like a sun. Their two young hearts
Beat with one note ; their twin and passionate souls,
Blent in desire stronger than time or death,

With tremblings born of rapture half perceived,
Unfolded wings immortal ; and upstood,
Poised on life's verge.   Their quickened sense per-
    ceived,
Though faint and far, that harmony of song
Which echoes through the spaces of the night
Up to the everlasting doors.   And, thus,
The tide of music flowing ; on their eyes
Eternal splendour breaking ; hand in hand,
Robed in their love and in their loveliness,
Without the ripple of a passing pang—
One perfect passion of immortal prayer,
They died before the God !

'Oh, Myrò, Myrô ! '

Myrô's sweet voice was silent, and the scroll
Slid from her slender fingers to the ground,
But, young Deinomaché—an April morn—
Burst into tears, and clasped the gentle hand.
Yet Myrô answered not.   Her far-off eyes
Gazed into distant mysteries, and sought
Vainly, it seemed, for answer ; and a storm
As if Athèna shook her aigis-fringe—
Swept o'er her spirit, and cast sombreness

Upon the solemn beauty of her face :
And the girl looked in wonder, mixed with dread,
To see it darken.   Thus a moment passed
That seemed an aeon : then the conquering soul
Shook her wings free, and grasped the nobler hope—
That never-failing weapon, whose bright point
Carves out a passage to eternal God
Through doubt and darkness ; and, upon her face,
There broke the radiance of a glorious smile,
Such as lights heaven and earth.   Deinomachè
Gazed as upon a goddess.   Then, once more
Spake Myrô, and her utterance, grave and sweet,
Thrilled to the soul, serene as highest Fate ;
A splendid passion, whose supreme control
Was godlike in its strength ; instinct with love,
Yet love made perfect in diviner light.
The discord, born of seeming failure, fled ;
And the warm Eros, who, we dreamed, had died,
Stood smiling tendernesses infinite.

' Yes, died before the God—the Power who reigns
And rules triumphant through all shocks of Time :
The Master of Love's loveliness ; the One—
The God Unknown, whose offspring we must be,
Who speaks in silence clearer than in sound.
He says, *I am ;* and we—His thirsty babes—
Yearn for the river of eternal love,

And feel towards the beauty that 'tis death
To gaze on.   But, that phantom of the dark—
Most useful in his office—cannot scare
The true God-seeking Soul.   The river, reeds,
And ferryman, and fish are nought.   The Two,
Tellis and Kleobeia, happy still,
And ever brightening in a broader bliss,
Pass through all portals to unmeasured peace.'

'Oh, it is sweet, but exquisitely sad!'

'Aye, my Deinomaché, I know thy thought.
Love and be loved, and let thy radiant eyes
Flash gleams like Aphroditê from the sea.
Be happy mother of a lion's whelp;
Reign more than queen : but, know, my comely Girl,
That through the ages, dotted here and there,
Sweet stars that will not bide the heat of day—
There are some souls, some lamps of purest fire,
Whom the gods cull to grace that fairer world,
Ere Time and all Time's littleness have dashed
Their virginal freshness.   They are Love's indeed :
His kiss awakes them to immortal life ;
They see his face, and they can ask no more.
He who has all is satisfied, and these
Nor marry, nor are married.   It is well.'

1895.

TO MR. AND MRS. GLADSTONE ON THEIR GOLDEN WEDDING.

Time ruined Paphos, but his rolling years
   Make love burn brighter; fifty winters chill
   And fifty summers, bringing good and ill,
Almost two generations' hopes and fears,
Pass into history; and yet our ears
   Receive the magic of thy voice, and thrill
   The nation's hearts. Fortunate statesman still
Close at thy side the loving wife appears.
If love can bloom so fair and last so long,
   Shall we not trust it on our future quest,
   And deem the better can but bring the best?
That lovely song must herald lovelier song?
So linked in golden bands, serene and strong
   Ye view the happy splendours of the West.

July, 1889.

II

In Memoriam

ALFRED, LORD TENNYSON,
POET LAUREATE.

SEE, the stately poet-prophet, he whose voice for sixty
    years,
Sweet, sonorous, patriotic, echoed through the nation's
    ears ;
With his life-work all accomplished, sung the song and
    fought the fight,
Whilst the noblest souls attest him as a true and stain-
    less knight,
Folds his warrior's mantle round him, yields at length,
    as all must yield,
And, by death proclaimed immortal, lies triumphant
    on his shield.
What a vista since the morning, since his earliest lays
    were sung,
Novel melodies and magic, when the century was
    young,
Vivid hope and faith of springtime ! Evermore will
    men recall
How your rainbow hues and splendours scintillate
    round Locksley Hall !

And, if years had chased some colour from the glory
    of that sky,

If the world had grown more sombre to the more
    experienced eye ;

Yet, remember that the Poet's faith in faith, and love,
    and truth,

Did but deepen with the shadows, mightier even than
    in youth ;

And, whilst wotting well the darkness which enwraps
    the struggling soul,

Knew that everlasting splendour is triumphant at the
    goal !

When his friend had passed the portal, how his spirit,
    pure and strong,

Faced the myriad doubts of sorrow, vanquished in
    melodious song :

Though the loved one died at sunrise, who a fairer
    fate can find?

Since, in sweetest aromatics, lies he evermore en-
    shrined.

How our Poet loved his country ! How he drew the
    perfect king,

Striving 'mid the world's wild winter to advance the
    touch of spring ;

Scorned, betrayed, deceived, forsaken, yet forgiving, as
    he goes

To that last stern sunset battle with his more than
    mortal foes ;

Call him Arthur—such a figure melancholy, sweet,
  sublime,
Shows the hero's godlike struggle with the agonies of
  time.
How our Poet bade us Britons, true to country and
  to throne,
With a soul unscared by danger, evermore to hold
  our own.
How he loved our English Harold, dauntless when
  the Norman came ;
How he loved our gentle Cranmer, more than victor
  in the flame !
How he viewed the shadowy ages with the poet's
  mystic sight,
Caught the Mantuan's subtle fragrance, grasped old
  Homer's ocean-might :
Every phase of life and being endless harmony im-
  parts ;
Sought he Nature, till the goddess took him to her
  heart of hearts,
Showed him secrets of her magic, taught him of her
  inmost ways,
Twined around his lofty forehead coronet of deathless
  bays.
Time was gentle—eighty winters could not tire his
  soaring flight :
Still his bow shot shafts of splendour through the
  darkness of the night.

But there comes a day when mortals from mortality
    must part ;
To the sacred Abbey bear him—lay him down on
    England's heart—
There to rest amid her great ones, not a merely formal
    fame,
But a memory that shall help us, and an everlasting
    name.
Now, whilst Britain stands in sorrow, gazing on the
    broken lyre,
Special joy and special sadness fit the Poet's native
    shire ;
Well he knew us, well he drew us, never can our
    hearts be cold,
We his humble kin who loved him, children of the
    fen and wold :
Dwellers where the fane of Lincoln high uplifts her
    matchless crest,
Where the stately tower of Boston stands a beacon in
    the west,
Where, beside the placid Welland, Stamford's ancient
    buildings lie,
Where old Barton's hoary churches tell the tale of
    long gone-by.
He shall stand in our Valhalla with our greatest past
    and gone ;
Langton, who the Charta wrested from the tyrant
    hand of John ;

Newton, whom divinest wisdom folded in a grand
 embrace,
Who revealed the mind Almighty to the furthest
 depths of space ;
Souls made perfect, they for ever with immortal
 beauty dwell,
Such as these, our county's heroes, such as these
 shall greet him well.
See, the gentle moonbeams falling, as he lies there,
 calm and pale,
Wrap him in their silvery splendour, earnest of the
 heavenly Grail ;
No unquiet bar was moaning when his Pilot, through
 the night,
Led his soul across the waters to the everlasting light ;
Where the poet's song is perfect, where the poet's
 hope is crowned,
Where the world's discordant echoes perish in melodious sound ;
Thought is music, music rapture, rapture love, and
 love divine :
And the harmonies eternal, deathless Singer, shall be
 thine !

October, 1892.

NEW YEAR'S HOPES.

Annus the year is Annulus,
 A ring of solar gold ;
Both joy and sorrow come to us
 Entwined around its fold :
  Heart sing free
  On the land or the sea,
And the singers unseen shall respond to thee.

Two angels in the heavens' employ
 Bore gifts, then passed again ;
And he was grave who left a joy,
 He smiled who gave a pain :
  Heart take these,
  Whether bitter or ease,
And thy bark shall not sink in the stormiest seas.

The Inharmonious dies away,
 The golden solar ring
Rolls onward to the perfect day
 Where all the Muses sing :
  Heart, no fear,
  For the true and the dear
Shall be joyous at last in that glad New Year.

December, 1888.

LIGHT AT EVENTIDE.

One more shadow on the dial,
One year less of storm and trial,
Patient hope and self-denial
    For life's guest.

And the trusting soul unshrinking,
With submissiveness is thinking
Of the glory slowly sinking
    In the west.

Still the sun in heaven is shining,
Yet his course may be declining,
And he leaves without repining
    Earthly jars.

Though, the evening gateway nearing,
We may see a radiance cheering,
In the silent, sweet appearing
    Of the stars.

Grant, life's path be somewhat shaded,
Grant, its brightest hues have faded,
There's a bloom dies not as they did
    In the past.

For love's Lord and high Defender,
Who preserves its blossom tender,
Shall reveal the flower in splendour,
                    At the last.

December 31, 1893.

THE DEATH-STROKE.*

'Twas the sunny Syrian sea
Off the coast of Tripoli,
    And the ironclads of England were at play
While their mimic thunder rent
With its roar the firmament,
    As they formed and they manœuvred in the bay:
For our navy is the pride
Of that sea without a tide,
    And our home is on the deep amid the spray.

Something terribly amiss
In a moment!   That or this,
    Man or mechanism?   Well, I do not know:
On the gallant flagship came,
Quick as stroke of lightning-flame

* Appeared in *The Academy*.

Or the giant rush of tempest, such a blow
That, her harness rent, she bowed ;
And, a mighty iron shroud,
　　With her Admiral and crew she sank below !

Do you deem they should have died
On a fierce and reddened tide,
　　In the fury and the glory of the fight ?
With the ensign shot to rags,
And with striking of the flags
　　Of the foemen on the left and on the right ;
With brave rescue from the wreck,
And wild cheering on the deck,
　　That Britannia had not parted with her might ?

Be such glory what it may,
Yet I venture still to say
　　That these shall not lose their guerdon or their
　　　　fame,
Though they died without a blow :
Well, the Highest—died He so ;
　　And our land shall shrine their memory and their
　　　　name :
For the man who, in the host,
Is death-stricken at his post,
　　' It is finished,' may triumphantly exclaim !

There is grief for me and you :
But for Tryon and his crew
   Happy future, as was honour in the past';
Though the Admiral no more
May hear wind or water roar,
   Though his sailors cannot battle with the blast,
For, the Pilot of all seas,
He will welcome souls like these,
   And shall guide them to fair haven—land at last !

June, 1893.

IN ROSAE HONOREM.*

It was at Thebes, the wedding-day
Of Kadmos and Harmonia ;
And all the Gods were there to grace,
   And all the Muses there to sing,
And all the little Loves that chase
   The hidden sweetness of the Spring,
Hastened o'er earth and air and sea,
To join in praise of Harmony—
     Divine, diviner Harmony.

* Appeared in *The Academy.*

Her lord in golden vestment dight,
  Her form the starry splendours deck;
For necklace fair, the gift of Night,
  Adorned the beauty of her neck.
I know this tale that men were telling,
  Speaks of the world in ordered grace,
As acted song and stately dwelling,
  Fit home for an immortal race;
Where all the varied parts that be
Inspire a note of harmony—
      Divine, diviner Harmony.

But yet, the basis of the whole
Is noble love of soul for soul;
Beyond the sway of stormy weather,
  Untouched by shock of mortal jars,
Where two clasp hands and stand together,
  And conquer darkness like the stars;
Whilst the sweet claims of me and thee
Wake myriad strains of harmony—
      Divine, diviner Harmony.

So, Kadmos, take thy Theban bride,
  Harmonia, ever fair and young;
But us the Gods have not denied
  The sweetness which their poets sung:

For, in our garden Love will stray
   To waken from their calm repose
A thousand flowers, that make it gay,
   And this fair morning culls a Rose ;
Bound in bright chain, yet ever free,
The two a link in harmony—
      Divine, divinest Harmony !

October, 1894.

TIME AND LOVE.*

SLY old Time took little Cupid,
   Tied a kerchief o'er his eyes ;
Turned him round, exclaiming, 'Stupid,
   Tell me where your true love lies.'
Long as moons shall shine above,
Time will play his tricks on love.

Cupid, of his power reminded,
   Showed old Time what he could do ;
And, that though his eyes were blinded,
   Yet his heart would guide him true.
Long as suns the heaven shall climb,
Love will foil the tricks of Time.

June, 1892.

      * Appeared in *The Academy*.

www.ingramcontent.com/pod-product-compliance
Lightning Source LLC
Chambersburg PA
CBHW020753020726
47495CB00008B/2412